Blue

AND OTHER STORIES
IN THE MANNER
OF ETHNOGRAPHIC BURLESQUE

William Young

ISBN 13: 978-1-7344236-2-4

Acknowledgements

THE AUTHOR GRATEFULLY acknowledges the following publications in which stories in Blue first appeared: Agni, Beloit Fiction Journal, Dark Horse, Prism International, Quarry West, Quarterly West, and Sequoia.

Table of Contents

Blue

"WE LITERALLY SPEAK a different language," he said to her, smiling.

She smiled back. He knew she didn't understand what he said.

"I mean I could talk to you until I'm blue in the face," he said—wishing at that moment he could turn his face blue—"and you wouldn't understand any better than you do right now. It's not that you're stupid"—he noticed that he was almost jeering at her—"just that you were born into another language. I could say anything I wanted to you right now. Anything at all, and you would keep smiling. Not that I would, of course" (she had cocked her head to the right a little), "I wouldn't think of it. It's not your fault, indeed I rather like it, that we speak such different languages."

"Fault?" she said. "California?"

He smiled. He was happy that she was his wife.

His friends had made fun of him when he'd gone to the agency, but once they got to know her they'd no doubt change their minds. They'd be jealous. Earlier in the day, when he'd made love to her for the first time, her body had opened like curtains.

So why was he almost jeering at her?

"Now you talk," he said. He moved away from the window—the sun was hot now—and sat down on the couch. "You talk," he said, drawing out the words so that she might better understand him. She didn't understand him.

"Farsi," he said, smiling. "Speak Farsi."

Her face lit up. She started talking. She was saying quite a lot. In Farsi. He didn't understand a word of it.

Although he did like its sound. The sound was nice. He could smell the curry in it. And there were figures on temples. Suddenly, she was swaddled in Indian blue and red and saffron yellow. She...

But she kept talking. She looked right at him, into his eyes, and kept talking. She didn't seem to realize that he didn't understand her. She was into it now. Yet he had the funny feeling that she was doing this on purpose. And after a while it wasn't music, and didn't smell good. The figures were strangling each other.

It reminded him of trying to read in Petite Boulangerie at lunchtime and being surrounded by women, by women talking. Talking over their entire lives. Not leaving out anything. As if he was interested in hearing every word of it. Almost as if they were talking to him, including him in their circle. All the details. How they felt about each little thing that had happened to them. What she had said and what he had said. How he had never grown up. "All he ever wants to do is ride his bicycle," he'd heard one woman say just the other day. Or, how he never pitches in. Or, he can't even pick the kid up from daycare. All he came there for was serious coffee, for a little peace and quiet, for a chance at the box scores, and instead they beat him over the head with a lot of talk these American women.

Why did they talk so much? What had gotten into them?

But this one he would love. They'd create a new language.

"Come," he said, stopping her talk. She followed him into the bedroom. "Undress," he said. To his surprise, she understood perfectly.

But he didn't want to just jump into bed. That would be too much like the old language.

He looked at her. Her skin was a beautiful shade of brown. Like rich wood. She stood before the bedroom mirror. Radiant. Shining, in the light from the window, like Isis. (She was looking into the mirror so that she could look out the window.)

So he too undressed. He removed his silk wedding shirt. Unfortunately, the old language, lust, came singing. But, he was trying. He walked up to her, from behind. He wanted to stand next to her, like husband and wife. Neither talking nor fucking. But she grabbed him. He looked in the mirror. And then he saw it. His body was blue.

Men

"Show me what you got," Danny said. The kid, eight or nine years old, stood on a bright red crate. Even then he could barely reach the speed bag. He was a white kid, probably from our neighborhood. Maybe a schoolmate had beaten him up. Maybe he was picked last for basketball games or something like that. Anyway, he did a good job on the speed bag. He made it blur. He had something. He might be able to stand in there with the black kids, or those Mexican boys from Danny's neighborhood. "Come back tomorrow at 3:30," Danny said. "After school. You go to school, don't you?"

That was the first time I'd laid eyes on Danny. I was as new to boxing as this kid. Danny was the head trainer at the gym. He was working there until he could turn pro. He was a hell of a boxer.

The kid was there early the next day. He was already there when I came for my three o'clock workout. He had a new pair of gym shorts; they were bright green and too big for him. "Timing, not power," Danny said to both of us and then walked away. Even when he walked his arms hung straight down at his sides. Meanwhile, the dummy head of the speed bag kept flashing out at me. It wasn't long before Danny had me in serious training. And it wasn't but a few months later that my marriage fell apart and I would up staying at his house.

After the speed bag, my routine usually called for jumping rope and work on the heavy bag. I wasn't ready for the ring, and I didn't have much. "Why do you want to take up boxing at your age" everybody said to me. I was thirty-five. "I guess I enjoy it," I would usually say back to them, but of course I knew it was more than that; I knew I was in training for something. I just didn't know what. And the club was convenient—only a mile from my office, across the wash and down Indian Bend Road. I can't tell you why a rich suburb like ours would choose to build a boxing club (sort of like Roxbury building polo grounds), but in today's world men don't learn to box and I think they're probably the worse for it.

Briefly, I'd taken up boxing as a kid. Had one bout in the basement of our house with my best friend, George Dietrich. But my braces made it an unfair fight. I was bleeding pretty good inside my mouth by the time I said I couldn't go on. No mas. "Look," I said, coming back from the bathroom, showing George, Tim, and Rick the inside of my mouth, which looked like bloody fish scales.

Danny would put on the mitts and we'd work on my combinations or, as was often the case, on foot work. Then it was back to the speed bag, which is good for reflexes. "A good boxer is someone who can slow time," Danny like to say.

Just about anything he said I believed. He'd never given me any reason to doubt him. I'd watched him in the ring. Like a lot of Mexican guys I'd seen, he had something real good. In Danny's case it was something special. In fact, I was there when he won the Arizona amateur lightweight title. I saw how something could be accomplished if you had a mind to do it. Danny had the support of his whole family. His wife and three kids and his parents and cousins, and a bunch of friends from his high school days in Guadalupe came to the bout. Danny won the title downtown in the Coliseum, where the Suns play. He wore white trunks— pantaloons blanco—and white shoes that night, and his long rat tail flipped around on the back of his neck as he bobbed and weaved. I sat right up front, next to his relatives. "Get'em, Danny. Get'em," I found myself yelling. I was up on my feet most of the fight. Danny's two boys—eight and six, I think they were—also were up and yelling. "Get'em, Daddy. Kill'em," his oldest, Michelangelo, yelled. Both boys were nicely dressed in black pants and white shirts.

Danny opened a cut under the black guy's left eye in the fourth, and then he went to work on that eye. He had a good left hook and a good jab. He'd devoted his life to learning the sweet science. Danny kept moving forward, his smooth, round shoulders jostling as again and again—his hands doing the shoeshine—he pounded his opponent. The cut was soon a gash, red and ugly. In the eighth the black fellow went down like a tranquilized animal. It took him a while to come to. Danny was dancing around the ring, but then suddenly stopped and kneeled down next to his victim. They shook hands in the end.

When Danny slipped through the ropes and came down to his family they kept hugging him. Even though he was sweating a lot, his skin shiny as butter in the high Coliseum lights, his family didn't hesitate to hug him. In fact, his father about squeezed the life out of him, Danny winking at me while clasped in his father's arms.

I unwrapped Danny's hands in the locker room. "Now we celebrate," he said. "You're coming with us, Whitey. One of my cousins has her eye on you. I told Maria you're married, but that didn't seem to bother her."

I had wanted my wife, Melanie, to come to the fight with me, but she wasn't interested. She didn't like boxing. In some respects it would have been nice for my daughter to have met Danny's kids, but neither me nor her mother had wanted her to see the fight.

So I went out with Danny's family. Met his cousin Maria. We had quite a few beers that night, spent a lot of money. Maria was a fun girl, with large breasts, as though a pair of boxing gloves were hid under her shirt. As it turned out, Danny paid for everything. But the next day he was back in the gym. So was that kid.

But it had been Melanie's idea in the first place. She didn't suggest boxing, she just suggested I do something besides work and play golf. Golf left her apoplectic. She thought it pretty silly for a group of grown men to drive around in a cart chasing a little white ball. "Furthermore, it makes your skin all splotchy," she said. "You're going to get skin cancer." I am blond and light skinned, nearly an albino. My given name is "Tom," but a lot of people call me "Whitey."

When I'd spend my Sunday watching golf on tv Melanie would just about scream, so I started watching the boxing instead. There was a lot on tv again—the most I remember since the Gillette Friday Night Fights in my youth. Since Floyd Patterson and Ingemar Johansson. ABC had lost professional baseball and college basketball to other stations so they'd started broadcasting fights (and bowling). And the Spanish station had a lot of boxing on, too, usually late at night—between rounds half-clad women climbed into the ring with placards. Often my daughter, Hartley, was around on Sundays but I'd tell her go upstairs or outside. I was always surprised to find that Hispanic families brought all the kids to fights. Danny had even brought his little girl to his title bout, although she slept through it. But a lot of times I've seen these little girls at ringside, watching their brother maybe. And of course a lot of times they'd see him get bloodied up. Sometimes, when boxing was on, Melanie would take Hartley shopping. We sort of split up the weekend, Melanie watching Hartley on Sundays and me on Saturdays. Saturdays, Hartley and I would go to the movies and to the park. She was smart kid and athletic. Once or twice I'd taken her to the club. She liked to spin the heavy bag, to watch it twirl—"like a ballerina in black tights," she said. Saturday was the best day of the week for me. It was nice to have time just for the two of us. I also wanted another child, but Melanie didn't.

Melanie did aerobics and tennis herself. She'd tried to get me interested in both of these activities, but I told her I wasn't interested. I let her know I didn't think either was for men, and of course she brought up golf and told me aerobics was a lot harder than it looked, and that it was good for your heart. I told her that when I was a kid there wasn't any such thing as aerobics, but I also told her that I did like to watch her do aerobics.

That is, I liked to watch her on those few occasions when I'd manage to be up by 6:30 in the morning or on those other days when she wouldn't get up in time for 20-Minute Workout and would play it that evening on the VCR when she came home from the hospital. In the mornings I asked her to do aerobics nude. She agreed to this request a couple of times, maybe three, and I had a real good time—watching her stretch and bounce around and how when she bent over the early light would shine across the room and sparkle on her moist backside. "Quite a bike rack you got there, honey," I remember saying to her on what must have been the third time she did it nude for me—the last time. She didn't appreciate my comment. Yet I wasn't able to hear what she said back to me (between breaths) because a plane happened to be flying over our house.

When we bought we didn't know we were in a flight path. Sky Harbor is downtown near the poor neighborhoods, but our suburban airport is getting larger and the planes flying in and out of there are bigger. Melanie thought this was something I should have looked into before we signed for the house. "I mean, you're the one that's from around here. You're the man," she said.

After a while I realized that no woman, especially one who works full-time and is pretty much exhausted and doesn't have much left, gets up at six in the morning to do aerobics for the benefit of her husband.

One day I walked into her office and found her talking intimately with her male assistant. He was a darkly handsome fellow, and well built. I told Melanie that very evening, after Hartley had gone to bed, that if I found out there was something funny going on between her and that guy I'd kick her out of the house. When we made love, later that night, I told her the same thing again. When we split up, soon after that, Melanie said something to the effect that she was going to get me back for all those times I'd gotten on top of her.

Danny still lived in Guadalupe, right off the freeway. Except for the freeway running high above the houses, the town hadn't changed much in the fifteen years or so since I'd last been there. In fact, they still called it the "Town of Guadalupe." Our Lady of Guadalupe Mission Church still stood, painted the same sparkling white, in the middle of town. Danny lived a block from the church, near the Circle B Drive Thru and radiator shop. Most of the houses had wooden fences but Danny's had a chain link fence. On the front of his house a carved wooden sign said "Trujillo." He said one of his neighbor's gave him that sign after he won the state title. He was a celebrity. "Hey, Danny, got a fight comin' up?" people said to him down there, in the same way they asked him that in the gym. The people of Guadalupe loved and respected Danny. Even his wife seemed a bit in awe of him.

I was awakened, that first morning away from my home, by the sound of a cock crowing.

"My best bantamweight," Danny said, handing me a cup of coffee. "Can't you feel it in his voice? Cock-sure of himself," he said, laughing. I laughed, too.

Danny was just out of the shower, wearing only boxer shorts. He looked ready for the ring. He had a fight coming up. He was working on making weight. His rib cage was visible, like the spine of a grilled salmon or some other anadromous fish.

Danny was doing what he could for me; he didn't understand "The Man" being allowed to throw me out of my own house on just my wife's say so. Luisa, also, was looking after me. She'd made a big breakfast: huevos and tortillas and fruit. Danny allowed himself a decent breakfast. He didn't eat lunch. At night he had a small, lean steak, a salad, and hot tea with lemon.

Danny and Luisa had a real family. They didn't have just one kid, they had three and wanted more. They didn't have much to live on, but they had something else, it seemed.

It wasn't until I watched their kids go off to school that the reality of what was happening to me began to sink in. Hartley, too, would probably be going off to school that morning, would be going off to school wondering where her dad was. When the Order of Protection was served on me I didn't know where to turn. Danny said I could stay with him and his family and I didn't hesitate. He and Luisa owned a small, three-bedroom adobe, passed down to them by her father. Luisa had grown up in the house. Now a full grown woman, a striking woman at that—features chipped from some soft, dark stone—it was odd to think of her running around that house many years earlier as a little girl.

When I'd first told Danny of my split from Melanie he hugged me, he said it was only one round of fifteen. He said I needed to be ready to go the distance. It was then that I knew I was going to make it through the ordeal. I knew that if I were patient, if I didn't lose my head, again, I'd have my daughter back and turn the tables on Melanie. I hated Melanie. I'd seen Danny in the ring and I'd been training and I knew if you wanted something bad enough and were man enough, if you could take and punch and wait for an opening, you'd be all right. He'd shown me that.

I was immediately to quit the premises, the Order of Protection had read. About an hour later Melanie called to say she wanted me out of the house right away. I asked her where she was and where Hartley was, but she wouldn't say, she wouldn't tell me. She said not to worry, Hartley was fine. She was safe. I'd be able to see Hartley after I moved out of the house. And remember, she said, you're not to damage anything on the way out.

But my first thought was to stay. No law could force me out of my own house just like that, right? Surely I at least had a trial coming to me. They'd have to break in and drag me out, was what I was thinking. I'll put the bookcase in front of the door. Unfortunately—or fortunately, as I now see it—I didn't have a gun. What really got to me, as I sat in my recliner thinking about it all, was that Melanie knew the Order of Protection was on its way and still slept in the same bed with me. For three nights she had slept with me—even had sex with me—as though nothing unusual was on the horizon. Melanie told the court that I had roughed her up, that I had slammed her against the wall. That I drank too much. All of this was more or less true–less than more–but what if it wasn't at all? The cops could still throw me out of my house upon Melanie's say-so.

I sat alone on Danny's front step and watched the Town of Guadalupe come alive–the children to school (most of them in what looked like Sunday best), the local people to their jobs, some of the women to cleaning their porches and yards (even raking the dirt)–and I realized suddenly and helplessly that my own life, or the life I felt I should be part of, was taking place far across the city, in a locality quite unlike Guadalupe. Here the roosters walked around in front of houses, a slight spring breeze rippled the Blackfoot daisies that bordered the fence, the sound of machines issued from the radiator shop next door. This was Danny's house, his world, not my own. I belonged in the suburbs, with my family.

Danny had gone off to work, to the gym. To another day of poorly paid work for my city. "You're welcome to stay here as long as you need to, Whitey," he'd said to me before leaving. Luisa too had gone off to her job.

Listen, your life can change as quickly as you change your shirt.

As I drove toward Desert Samaritan everything I saw, everything around me suddenly appeared strangely alive and meaningful. Life seemed vivid and coherent. All the colors before me–the violet of South Mountain, the sparkling desert lawns–moved like a sea. I thought of Hartley, how blond she was, almost as light as I am. Thrust from my world, the universe itself seemed to listen in on and respond to my thoughts. The world looked complete and whole and real. I felt like a man. For perhaps the first time in my life I felt like a man. And surely it was that feeling, the adrenaline rush of the universe entering my veins, that made it so easy to go to Melanie's office and settle things with this male assistant of hers. Surely something had caused him to be in her office at that precise moment, when time slowed for me, when I caught him flush with the left hook Danny had taught me. There was some mysterious justice at work.

He fell across her desk like a supplicant.

My only regret is that when I awoke in the morning, when dragged from my cell at daybreak to face the judge, my hands cuffed behind me–"Put your palms together facing each other," the officer said, "makes it easier for you"—my regret is that Danny was there, too, hauled in on a separate and unrelated charge. Drug running. We six men stood together. One guy, who had neglected to appear at the hearing for failure to own an urban fishing license, was naked from the waist up—maybe he didn't have a shirt to change into! We six stood together awaiting the recitation of the charges against us. We six, all men. Myself; Danny; the half-clad guy, who was undoubtedly the one who'd been up all night talking about how wacked out he was on LSD, another guy, well dressed, and like me from the neighborhood; and finally two Mexican nationals, who either couldn't or wouldn't respond to questions put to them in English.

These latter two had been brought in on charges of underage drinking and disorderly conduct. Neither had a green card. One claimed to not even know the name of the person he worked for. He worked on a lawn crew. I felt like I'd seen him around our area; I couldn't be sure. "Is there a name on the side of the truck?" the judge asked. It was a pretty smart question. A $150 bail was set for each of these nationals. $25 for the fisherman. The local was released O.R. As was I, despite the assault. "Everything about you points to the feeling that you're not the kind of person who would normally do such a thing," the judge said. "This sounds to me more like a domestic matter than a criminal one. Since you have ties to the community, you are released, for now, without bail."

Danny is still in County, pending trial. We talk through the screen. Sometimes Maria comes with me. "How's that kid doing?" Danny never fails to ask. I tell him he's doing fine. "He can still make it blur. He asks about you," I say, as Danny, self-conscious, looks down at his hands. I visit him every other weekend, the weekends I don't have Hartley.

The Extremities

Before she shot off her right foot, Molly moved about slowly but with paced determination, stalking her life like a trapper. Since the "accident," she hobbled a little. Her short, stout body moved crisply, now, still, but there appeared a slight falter every third step, as though her body could stand the body weight blow only one time out of two.

When the sun came up, no matter the pain in her foot, Molly had to feed the chickens. She lived in a yellow school bus, her temporary home while she finished building her new house. She got up, splashed water on her face and neck, shook dandruff from her red, bushy hair, then fed the damn chickens. There was no forgetting them, no sleeping in, because, simply, the cock did crow each morning as soon as he spotted the thin, bright line of the coming day. The rhythm of the morning, for Molly, was not flowing, but precise, scheduled. She liked it that way, as long as the schedule was nature's or her own. She didn't care to follow someone else's idea of the way time worked. Once, a year before, she'd followed her husband's ideas, and for a while she was happy. But, after many threats, her husband finally left her. Molly moved back to the countryside, bought land, and set to building her house. Occasionally friends came by to hold a board or help lift heavier materials, but mainly Molly built up the house herself. As fall and the Northwest rains closed in, she prepared to slap on a roof. Her house wasn't much bigger than the bus, but the house, by virtue of its wheel-lessness, already felt more like a home.

Molly accepted a lack of negatives as positive, until the time came to embrace a positive again. Of course, this meant a man. It did, she didn't kid herself. She liked men and believed, no matter the shit she'd gone through with Larry, that she would find a man who would want to live with her and love her. She hoped he would be more worldly than she was. She was a mountain woman–woodchopper, musician, babymaker and nurser (someday), feeder of chickens, all wonderful things she could do, after years of upbringing. Molly would wear a skirt from him, if he wanted her to, on occasion.

She had a man in mind. He was coming for lunch. She fed the chickens, made herself a light breakfast, coffee and a bagel, chopped the firewood, and sat down to practice her mandolin. It was Sunday, a beautiful clear mountain Sunday. Molly Kowalski didn't build on Sunday, because of herself, not because of God. She needed the rest, and she wasn't a Catholic. Larry was Polish Catholic and Molly hadn't changed her name back, yet. Everyone thought she was Catholic, however–Irish if not Polish–and they treated her as though by living alone in the mountains she sought escape from her Catholic family, with its expectation of marriage and children, or they thought she was becoming a nun/monk in her own way. But her maiden name was Olsen. She hadn't been raised in a church and liked the Northwest because nature superseded and trumped religion. Nature was itself, good and bad, but religion was a negative twisted toward a positive, and Molly feared the way things became twisted.

The sound of the mandolin filled the valley with Baroque music. The calluses on her fingertips were returning. She hadn't played during her one-year marriage, hadn't any desire to, but the quiet of her new life, interrupted only by the noise of the hammer and saw, needed some mediator, a sign of life between the valley winds and the sound of construction. It was nice to sit back and play, with the weight off her bad foot. Molly thought about Billy, her visitor for lunch (or was it "dinner" on Sunday). This was the third Sunday in succession that he would come. A few times he'd shown up late at night, drunk and apologetic, and then fucked her in a rough-beast fashion. He said the night air caused his roughness. She wasn't so sure about that, but liked the effect–and the vision of her bus rocking like a boat at dockside. Lately he had become gentler, and she was as pleased by the gentle lovemaking as by the rough. She compared it all to the wind and the hammer, but again she knew she needed something more, something between.

Sunday afternoons were especially nice. On the warm August afternoons he would strip off his shirt, pull off her shirt as well, and then grab two baseball mitts from the trunk of his car. "We're heading toward World Series time, Molly," he'd said last week, "the whole season comes down to a few games."

They played in the sunshine, bare chested, for a good hour. His thin, sinewy-strong body was fluid and beautiful. Molly felt short and a little stocky, and she was happy to have someone, if only once or twice a week, who had grace and sleek form. He was, also, very theatrical. He liked to mimic professional pitchers. He had a an elaborate but compact delivery—fingertips to the mouth, a tip of his baseball cap (marked "Cleveland Indians"), followed by the shaking on and off of signs (fastball, curve, slider, spitter)—until finally he'd whip it to her, straight and hard, expecting her to play like one of the boys. As the "season" progressed, she'd learned to use the mitt with more felicity. She could catch the ball in the pocket, as well as the webbing, with only a slight sting.

Against the backdrop of the coming fall colors, his white car turned and twisted up the dirt road sewing a tapestry. And then, suddenly, he was there. He leaned out the driver's side window.

"Damn nice to see you, Molly. Been a coon's age."

Molly sat on her bus steps. "So you've come to make fun of us mountain folk."

"Not me. I'm serious as a hog at the slop."

He laughed and swept his brown hair away from his forehead. She knew they kidded each other at first because their relationship was still unclear. They called it companionship and sex. Each meeting was a good but pretty separate thing. They talked more frankly as time went on, and at times eased up on the sexual violence, but there was no definable progression or leaps of faith. "I is your city boy, you my country woman," he'd said more than once. He emphasized his boy-ness versus her womanness, even though they were both closing in on thirty. She had a premonition that he was living out some fantasy.

"I could use a haircut," he said, exiting his car.

"Why? Let it grow. Don't ever shave..."

"Become a man?"

"It might add an inch here and there," Molly said.

"I like to make you work to have fun."

"I'll get the scissors, Billy."

She climbed to the back of the bus. She knew right where the scissors were laid.

"How much off?"

"An inch? I'm not particular."

"And the back?"

"Cut it into some pattern—a baseball diamond. My right ear is first base, my..." He stopped talking.

"What?" she asked, noticing his agitation.

"My voice carries too far in this valley. I can hear myself and I don't like it. The echo."

Molly wanted his voice to fill the valley more regularly. He cut a nice figure there on the bus steps, his back erect and his head still. Clipped, thick, dark hair fell onto his bare shoulders. She wondered about how it would begin this time, before dinner or after, in the grass or in the bus, or in her almost finished house. She would let him decide, take her.

"I think that's enough," Molly said. "You don't want to look like the gays or punk rockers, do you? I'll get the mirror."

When she returned with the mirror he pulled her down to him by her right ankle. She swallowed. The pain spread through her foot like lightening through the sky. She felt him rub up against her, from behind. She leaned forward, steadied by her hands on the floor of the bus, just above the steps. The mirror lay flat.

"I like to watch," he said. "In the city you can see your reflection in everything, windows, street signs, cars." Billy lived in Vancouver, having run from the draft. He set the mirror against the bus door, where the mirror reflected their faces, his face draped on her neck.

Molly wasn't too keen on watching. Mirrors, even the lake down the road, frightened her. She didn't like the look of her face and his slanted and distorted in the glass. Still, she stood it, bent over, didn't mention it, let him undo her gold belt buckle. It began that way, on the bus steps, standing, rough-shod fashion.

"Okay?" he said, tugging at her jeans.

"Yes, okay," Molly said. She was afraid to say no. Afraid he would never come back, and afraid of saying no to him.

Billy opened her shirt and cupped her breasts. His pants were down. She marveled at his ease and speed. As his cock came under her she looked at the mirror, and at the butt of her gun, poised behind the folded yellow bus door. The pain in her foot, in the upright position, was extraordinary. She knew what she did.

Jesus, did she. But it was better than the domestic bed with the weight off her foot, a better mixture of pleasure and pain. Billy argued that one could not truly live without forcing one's self to the limits of tolerance. "There is only one way out of the middle-class mess, pushing to the edge. Pushing back the frontiers," he'd said the first time they'd met, as though he had to state his position toward life from the start.

"I am not exactly living in the middle of the middle-class mess," Molly had responded.

"But your mind is. Your mind, Molly."

So Molly, entertaining the truth of his arguments, was persuaded to give up the battle and give her body. She would let him do what he wanted, let him manipulate her, as long as he performed. She'd submit; perhaps she was a strange Catholic. She laughed at this thought, her teeth shining in the mirror, just as he entered her.

He was very hard, this time. Often he wasn't, at first. It took a couple or three strokes, and usually a little roughness, before he truly stiffened and hit a good rhythm. He stroked; she watched him watch himself in the glass; she felt him swelling inside her.

"Don't come yet, Billy," she said.

"I can't stop," he said, pumping harder, sweating.

She tried to pull away. "Then don't do it at all," she said, surprised by her words.

They separated, and she turned and sat down on the steps. His cock pointed at her like a gun. Molly thought of the night—the drunken night—she'd shot off part of her foot. She wasn't clear, even now, whether she had meant to do it. She had just wanted to do something.

Billy took her hands and spread them at her sides. He held them flat, brought his body to hers. She struggled. This time she didn't want it so hard and fast, but her struggling only encouraged him. He smiled, forced her hand back flat, rubbed his cock on her stomach. He appeared possessed by the idea of having her, one way or another.

"Quit it. I don't want to."

He stopped. "Really?"

"I don't. Really." He let go.

"Why?"

"I don't." Molly gasped, started to cry. Her thick body shook. "Crying is something I don't do," she said, at last. "Something I don't do."

Billy brought his head gently to her chest, paused, and then raised his head again. "I have come to bring you to things you don't do," he said, dramatically.

His look startled her. He looked empty behind his blue eyes, only a glass image of a person. Why did he talk like that? She realized that her attraction to him was dangerous—that, in some sense, he had been a cause for pulling the trigger. She had wanted him there more often and longer. To possess him as he possessed her. But she saw what she wanted, after all, was the smoothness of his form, not what lay beneath. Molly was frightened to think how far she had traveled from her original desires, how easily twisted her mind became when she was alone in the mountains. She saw the idiocy of rural life as she'd once seen the madness of city life. She felt a little like screaming, but it seemed the valley would swallow not echo her sounds.

"You must accept," he said. "Not fight me. You must be willing or it won't take, as hypnosis won't take. I can bring you to your extremities, from your bowels to your extremities and way beyond, but you must be willing—a willing woman. You must accept my violence, my gentleness. In between and you do not live fully."

"Don't talk like that," Molly said. "You just want control," she said. But it was a new voice, disembodied. She sounded like him, thin, metallic. He did not want real fire, only control or self-immolation. He had run from the war, but there was something, in him, that wanted destruction. Yet, what she said was not true because she wanted her bowels set on fire, her cunt plunged—she wanted his smooth body to spread its warmth to the extremities of her body. She had lied and sounded like him.

"Do what you want then," Molly said. She couldn't bare to think of him going for good, disappearing, like water from a creek bed. She had realized her great distaste for her solitary, mountain life. She was like a nun building a private chapel. "Go on, then," she said. She leaned back on her hands, spread open her legs. Her red pubic bush shown in the sunlight. "Go on, go on," she said, like a chant. He moved to her, leaned on her, then he reached behind the bus door for the shotgun.

He set the shotgun next to the mirror, the black, smooth bore of the gun aimed at their heads. She knew it was loaded. Larry had killed her belief; Billy brought her a kind of sickness– now he made the whole damn thing feel unreal.

"We must move quietly so we don't set it off," he said. "But we must, at the same time, fuck as hard as we can, smoothly, silently, as though we were a soundless film. As though we existed only as a movie. A sex and violence movie," he added.

Directed by a little fascist, she thought, as he entered her once more. He drove up into her. She gasped, but, eyeing the gun, kept herself still. He liked her that way anyway. When she moved her hips too much he slipped out, couldn't find the right rhythm. She lay still. Raised up above her, he drove harder and harder, his cock straight as a ruler. The pain in her foot diminished.

"Oh, Molly," he cried, his face bobbing in front of the gun barrel. Bobbing, and bobbing, he moved above her; she felt caught below like a fish. She could feel him swell, feel a warmth spread in her cunt. He worked with precise passion. At last, he came. And she came with him. She slumped to the floor of the bus. He pulled his shrunken penis out, and sat on the bus steps. Then, he began to laugh. Resignedly, with a touch of hysteria, he laughed. "The gun had to go off. Should have gone off," he said. "But it didn't. I came all this way from Cleveland and it didn't go off. That's the damn Northwest for you."

Molly drew in a breath, regained her lost voice. "What are you talking about?"

"No violence. Just calm and meditation–quiet daily rain. It's a great joke on those of us who move out here looking for raw, rough life. The Wild West. Instead, this place is a dark, little Scandinavia. No frontier for miles."

"You might be surprised," Molly responded. He looked nervous, glazed. "Maybe surprised...but not you, eh? You don't like surprise and spontaneity. You like outrage and control, don't you Billy? You like to make things unreal, surreal, because you won't let life take you to its senses and dangers. To real extremes. Which is probably why you attract me, or did. You don't give a damn about life."

Billy looked at Molly, perhaps a little hurt and surprised by her comments; but nevertheless he kept laughing. He laughed through his nose. His pants were still at his knees.

Molly, who sat on the bus steps, completely naked, thought he looked not only silly, but scared and frozen, emotionally frozen. She wanted him to leave. "Go on, now," she said to him, "go on."

"I'm going," he said, and then, suddenly, was long gone.

As Billy's white car twisted and turned down the road into the valley and toward the city, Molly packed. She took a bottle of burgundy, a bedroll, the shotgun, and moved into her unfinished house. She laid out the bedroll, opened the wine, and watched as the light from the sunset curved and spread throughout the valley, like the hand of a god. The rhythm of the evening moved across the land and filled her with a strange and slightly frightening elation. She would kill herself during the night or wake in the morning and build a roof, alone. She knew those two extremes smacked of Western melodrama, but she couldn't picture anything else, anything in between.

Only later that cool August night, when the pain in her foot lessened, and she set to playing her mandolin, did she feel more hopeful.

River Rats

HE WAS IN the small dental office so he was warm after the snow but too warm. He wanted to take his parka off, which he'd put on over a sweater. He stood up and hung the parka on the wooden coat rack and sat back down next to his mother. A day he'd long wanted to avoid had arrived. His mother had picked him up earlier at the junior high, he having waited alone in the "C" wing while everybody else was in class. The snow drifts beyond the door were turning white-blue in the fading afternoon sun. He and his mother had stopped briefly at home so he could brush his teeth. The dental office was on the levee on the other side of town, the East Side–down the hill and across the Wabash from his family's home ground, the West Side.

With its small windows and musty smell the dentist office was not what he'd pictured beforehand.

"Where's the aquarium like in new offices?" he'd said to his mom.

"He's supposed to be a good orthodontist," Mrs. Severall said, glancing up from her magazine.

She had promised to have him back to school in time for basketball practice. He'd be missing his usual rendevous with Cathy in any case. Their habit was to sequester themselves for ten minutes or so near the trophy case when school let out. He'd linger so much at times that most of the guys would be already dressed for practice when he got there–though Morrissey, like Jack, often ran late, and they'd dress out together. Or sometimes it was Boyd, whom he didn't like. They'd fought once at practice, Jack acquiring a certain rep for taking on a bigger guy but having never revealed that he knew the fight would be broken up by the coach before any damage was done.

He wasn't sure what Cathy might have scheduled: maybe a club meeting or Student Council. She'd had on that gray, wool crew-neck which went so well with her green eyes. She'd eat lunch with her girlfriends on the other side of the cafeteria. Fortunately he'd have extra time with her at the varsity basketball game Friday night, against their big rival, Lafayette Jefferson.

He was both in a hurry and not to start the dental exam.

"Come on in, son," Dr. Marsden said, appearing suddenly from behind the reception desk. He wore the standard-issue white coat, but he was an old man, no one's picture of a dentist. Jack was to look over at his mom as if to say to her, "Boy, this guy is a geezer"–but she didn't seem to get his drift. Immediately a young woman–"May," said her name tag–appeared as well and showed him to a small room, the gleaming white dentist chair like a landed spaceship dominating the office. Dr. Marsden had gone into another room. Then May was gone, too. Out the window, the river, brown as a squirrel, snow aside its banks, presented itself (the street snow already a dirty white, the gutter like charcoal).

Dr. Marsden came back in the room and fiddled with his instruments, May preparing a compound. She was attractive–probably an East Side girl, who would be unlikely to go on to Purdue but would someday make some man happy, as they liked to say. She was small and dark- haired like his own Cathy. He looked at her teeth: they were perfect, shiny. But why had his mom chosen Doc Marsden, Jack was wondering? And why the East Side?

His mom had been insistent that he have braces, "Even if it means taking out a second mortgage on the house." He'd heard her arguing with his father about it at the time. "Money didn't grow on trees" was a phrase he often heard repeated.

"Jackie doesn't need braces," his father saying.

"Maybe fine for Caldwell, Ohio," his mother said, working in a kind of slam at his dad's farmer's heritage, though in fact his father had grown up in Cleveland a professor's child and was an engineering Ph.D.

Jack had an overbite.

Marsden hands were liver-spotted. And his ears and nose were much bigger than his shrunken, splotchy, gargoyle-like face. Eighty if he was a day.

"How are you, young man?" Marsden had said. "Just preliminary this afternoon. Some x-rays."

In her rubber-gloved hands, May was holding two white tong-like shapes made of Indiana limestone. She handed them to Dr. Marsden.

"Now, son, I want you to put one of these in each corner of your mouth and pull your mouth as wide apart as it will go. Real wide. Got that, my boy?"

"Yes, sir," Jack said.

"May here will help you."

She offered a sympathetic smile. And showed him how to use the tongs, although there was nothing to it really. Just stretching your mouth as wide open as possible. Jack was thinking about his mother, wondering if she'd maybe started up a conversation with someone in the lobby, when all of a sudden he saw her standing in the doorway, right behind Dr. Marsden. His mother was a beautiful woman, and unlike a lot of woman in town kept her hair—she was brunette—girlishly long and straight. Apparently she wanted to see for herself what was going on, see what she was paying for, what the $800 was going for.

"Now pull it apart as far as you can, son," Dr. Marsden said.

May helped.

"No, wider," Dr. Marsden said. "It's not going to rip open. Now hold it just like that."

Marsden shot the x-rays patiently—way too slowly, it seemed to Jack, the x-ray machine unwieldy, like the big TV cameras on Dinah Shore or Perry Como.

"Think of something pleasant," May said, lightly touching his forearm. "Think of something else. We're almost through," she said.

He dutifully tried to think of something else. First, Cathy. Then for some reason he thought about cornfields, of the way that when you were driving by them they looked like a Japanese fan or an accordion. But that thought led him to thoughts about his job over the past summer working in the cornfields, detassling corn, walking up and down the long straight white- yellow rows in the sweltering heat. He and Morrissey were the only West Siders among the group of boys. The first day on the farm-bus some crosstown kid had gone for his lunch bag—something he would never forget—and instinctively he had pushed the kid away and grabbed it back. From then on things were pretty clear, the lines drawn. He had their respect. But two weeks into the job his father, who didn't teach in the summer, announced they were going on vacation, to Florida. Morrissey not so lucky for the rest of the summer presumably.

Jack looked up at his mother and Dr. Marsden and May.

"Wider," Dr. Marsden said.

It indeed seemed odd to be at basketball having not first spent some time in the hallways with Cathy. But he'd see her at school tomorrow and then the Jeff game. The schools weren't allowed to play football against each other—too many fights—but everybody knew basketball was what counted anyway. West Side rarely beat Jeff, a bigger school, a state powerhouse. Lafayette Jeff could beat the likes of Gary and Muncie and Indianapolis Manuel. But beating "the River Rats" was their greatest desire.

The whole town had come to the game, the cheerleaders scarcely having room to operate. The high school kids—who seemed sort of like gods—cheered and stomped their feet on the bleachers. Most of the boys wore letter sweaters or their girlfriends wore them. The sweaters were gray cardigans with a big scarlet WS on the front. His brother's letter sweater was adorned on the shoulder with a basketball and a tennis racket. Most of the cheers intended one form of insult or another. The game was an hour of cheering and stomping and standing up and Jack had happily joined in. Jeff won. But the thrill, the penumbra, of the game—a close one—still hovered over the crowd as both sides slowly filed out of the packed gym. His older brother, Bryce, who was on the Varsity, hadn't played however, due to the game's gravity.

In the entryway Jack waited for Cathy, who'd gone into the little girls room for a minute. The snow had started up again. The snow was ubiquitous in the dark, like atomic fallout. It was a wet snow. He wasn't wearing boots. As a kid, against his mother's wishes, he would leave his black rubber boots outside the door of the house, putting them on again when he returned from school—even rubbing snow into the silver buckles for authenticity.

"Hey, young Severall," Mr. Mack suddenly called out. Mack was the woodshop teacher at both the high school and the junior high. "Where's your wife?"

Wouldn't you like to know, Jack thought to himself, as he waved.

Cathy had come out the bathroom but was talking to the Van Natter twins, both cheerleaders for the junior high team. He liked Charlie better than Alex because the former was shy. They both had bright red hair though.

Cathy looked great. Along with the gray sweater she wore a black wool skirt and high tan leather boots with faux-fur around the tops.

"Where's your boots, Jack?" she said, noticing his tennies. "You'll just freeze." She pulled the hood of her black parka over her head.

"I'll be fine," he said, as they made their way outside, out from the crowd, onto Meridian.

"We almost beat them, huh?" Cathy said.

"The depth of their bench made the difference, especially Shepherd. He didn't score much but played good defense on Horse. And Paddy Brady was Paddy Brady, just as expected. He scored eighteen, I think."

"You know a lot about basketball, don't you?" Cathy said, inching up close to him.

Her eyes were lit by the falling snow in the streetlights.

Jack was trying to keep his teeth from chattering. He put his arm around Cathy, which was the most he'd ever done at any time with her. He'd never kissed her–she didn't seem like the kind of girl you kissed, or fondled, though he did want to, and soon.

"You haven't talked about the dentist?" she said.

"Not very romantic, I guess."

"I've heard Doc Marsden is way behind the times. Like going to an old dudgeon, it is. A torture chamber."

"It wasn't so bad," Jack said, although in truth his jaw was still sore. He'd taken two aspirin before the game. "But I hadn't heard what you heard," he added.

"He's cheaper though, I've heard," Cathy said.

"Is he?"

"That's what my mom said. She's just glad that I don't need braces."

Cathy's family was poorer than some others on the West Side. Her father was staff at the university while his father was faculty. Her father probably made about the same as Tommy Morrissey's dad, though she was an only child and the Morrisseys were nine altogether. The Morrissey twins, boys, slept in the attic.

Jack that night planned to kiss Cathy, come hell or high water. Over the summer and into the early fall he'd sat with her for hours at a stretch on her front porch and they'd talked and talked–kidding each other a lot and looking into each other's eyes. But he'd never made his move. And sometimes he thought it might be her fault. Even in the long wordless pauses, when there was only the sound of traffic and birds and wind, it wasn't entirely clear to him that she'd signaled her willingness.

But if he didn't kiss her soon, it would get too hard, too awkward to do it ever. And if he didn't kiss her he'd never get a piece. He was dying to feel her up, the way he'd done it one time to Alex Van Natter at a party when someone turned the lights out. Jack always wondered if Alex had told Charlie–if they told each other everything. It would be like feeling up Charlie, too.

He sat down with Cathy under the yellow porch light, his teeth still chattering a bit. His feet were soaked through. He'd manfully kept the hood of his parka off on the walk to Cathy's house and so now his head too was wet from the snow. His feet and head were wet and cold. But right then he didn't care. He looked at Cathy. Her small, bright face was half-hidden under the hood of her parka. Perhaps she would get mousey someday, but right then she was beautiful, perfect. He thought back on the fight with Boyd.

"Do you like Boyd?" Jack suddenly blurted out.

"What? What are you talking about?" said Cathy.

"Boyd?" she said.

"Never mind. I've seen him eyeing you. I just thought maybe..."

"Don't even say it...hold me.'

Jack held her, and he put his cheek next to hers, a gesture more familiar than kissing. But then he did kiss her. He French-kissed her, moving his tongue all around, and his hand inside her parka touched her outside her sweater. Then– thinking, the hell with Boyd–he slipped his hand underneath her sweater and touched the most reachable breast. Then the other.

There was still the walk home, four blocks in the dark. But it was a safe neighborhood and Jack was feeling terrific, supercharged up.

In any case, he walked in the middle of the street—it was drier, and should a dog happen to jump out from one side or the other he'd have more time to react. Before going in the house he stood outside for a minute and looked around. The bright orange moon, like the head of a giraffe, was slowly emerging from behind the silhouettes of the trees on the ridge. Even the junior high, which was right above their neighborhood, was now bathed by the light.

His youngest brother was already asleep. His older brother wasn't home and Cary, closest to Jack's age, was in the basement watching TV. Their dad had paneled the basement, made it into a family room. He'd even built-in a neon, simulated waterfall behind the ping-pong table—the "water" fell continuously. Still, since the real water pipes were exposed and the windows at the top of walls were so small you couldn't altogether forget that is was a basement.

His mom was in bed, reading. His father was sitting at the kitchen table, pouring through the newspaper. Sundays they got the Indianapolis Star but otherwise it was the Lafayette Journal and Courier.

"Quite a game tonight, Jackie, wasn't it," his father said. "Too bad Bryce didn't get a chance to play." Though his father didn't much care about sports, Jack could tell his dad felt bad for Bryce. "Want something? Some ice cream? Vanilla, your favorite. Put some chocolate sauce on it and make it good."

The last comment was a kind of joke on his father's part: the family sometimes made fun of their father's love of dessert, of his unsophisticated Ohio ways.

As for Bryce, he was off to Vanderbilt in the fall, so he'd be all right. He'd won a scholarship, though Vanderbilt would still be a financial burden on the family.

"Brownie?"

Jack looked at his father.

"I'm fine, Dad."

"Well, sit down for a minute anyway. I've got something to tell you. Something you should know."

It must be important. His father never sat him down for a heart-to-heart. If they were moving away somewhere, if he was going to have to give up Cathy, he felt for sure he would kill himself.

"I've got some sad news, Jack. I've just been reading that Dr. Marsden died yesterday. His obituary is in the paper here. Do you want to read it?"

"He's dead?"

"Died yesterday morning."

"How strange," Jack said, drifting off.

He'd been with him, Dr. Marsden, the day before he died. It was almost like being touched by dead hands.

He looked at his father.

"I think I'll go to bed, Dad," he said. "I'm sorry about Doc Marsden."

He shared a room with Cary—who slept with his eyes half open—but at Jack's request his father had built a half-partition in the room. Older, he got the side away from the door. There was even talk about building an addition onto the back of the house. Jack was next in line for a room of his own. Cary would have to double up with Curt.

Anyway, Cary was downstairs watching TV. Their mother had probably fallen asleep.

His father had turned down the heat, so the bedroom was cold. Only the bathroom was kept warm. Jack undressed quickly and slipped naked under the covers, the covers crackling with static as he climbed in. He thought about the kissing he'd done with Cathy, his hands on her breasts, working the two nipples. Now, he'd be able to kiss her and touch her whenever he wanted. And he'd be going to a different orthodontist—probably, despite the additional expense. He wouldn't see May again. He wouldn't see Boyd until Monday, fortunately.

But he felt he'd shown Boyd and everybody.

Winter Fishing

1

I washed the windows today. The distance between these windows and those across the way has been dredged, like a river, of ancient pollutants. A new snow has fallen upon the ledges under the windows and I can almost see the individual flakes. She's due home from work at four. I wonder if she'll notice?

This hasn't been going on very long. I moved in in November; she was the only bright spot in a long, sickly gray month. I'd do the chores, work a little on my thesis (on Heidegger), and, suspendedly animated, a character in cinema verite, wait for her return, thinking perhaps she'd surprise me and come home early. But she never comes early. I sit in the livingroom, the afternoon Globe folded upon my knee like a napkin, and wait for her to appear wrapped like an animal in her fur coat. I've done the laundry, washed the dishes. The laundry machine in the basement stole three quarters of mine so I had to go down to the corner and sit with several women while the machines roared, demanding more quarters, never satisfied, though perhaps somewhat spent at the end. I do not like to go out in the daytime. I did four loads, all the clothes, sheets, and towels in the apartment.

Fortunately, she cooks. I like to watch her cook. There are a thousand little movements I like–the elbow raised to pour the salt, the reaching up above the counter for another sauce pan. But the best part comes before the food. Ever since she realized that I like to watch, she dresses and undresses for me in full view, displaying her charms. I've had a few drinks by that time and see her through the nice fog of my inebriation. Her entire body naked, wet from the shower, she rubs herself until I can almost see the red glow. She dries her hair with quick, electric motions of the towel. The day is long, and I always wait for her to come in.

It started when I'd dress for her in the morning. I'd get up about an half an hour before she'd arise, put on the coffee, and then take a long, hot shower. Water is one thing included in the rent, and I do abuse it.

I've learned to dress slowly because she watches for as long as I take, up until eight-thirty when she leaves for work. I, too, used to go out into the deep snow of the working world, but slowly, oddly, I felt myself helplessly pulled away, indoors. It is good that, like Kierkegaard, I have a trust fund.

I've begun to wonder what she does for a living. She dresses colorfully–purple, orange, red, often in satin. I think she's a New Waver. But she doesn't let me watch in the morning, just appears full-blown, dressed, luminescent as an exotic fish. Yet this day is different. She watches my exaggerated performance, my clown's pantomime. I parade naked about the room, ostensibly trying to decide what to wear. I pull out a shirt, try it on, take if off, and put it back. I try several pairs of underwear, searching for the right fit! One day I returned from the shower my cock erect as a Canadian Mountie–I imagine she got a kick out of that. I try to keep things interesting. Take different poses. Bend over in front of my dresser. And this day, the day after I'd washed the windows clean of filth, she dresses for me in the morning, too. Her red bathrobe drops to the couch. She opens the refrigerator door and I can see more clearly the gift she offers. She bends to the shelf for eggs or milk or butter, and the cleft of her buttocks cuts neatly across my vision. Ah, I am happy to have this other hour with her. This and the hour we share before he returns at five.

3 p.m. The day is long to him who is awake. I put away my thesis– "Being and Becoming in Heidegger's Being and Time." I have spent several hours in the stacks of the city library, trying to concentrate on the task at hand. But I got off the train track. There is nothing so erotic as a library...save the vision from my livingroom. Some people virtually live at the city library, all their belongings stacked upon a desk. And, of course, some cruise the basement floor bathroom.

There's an occasional baglady, but mostly it's men. Alcoholic men. The great pitiful race of men!

I wound up reading Havelock Ellis on voyeurism and exhibitionism. But it didn't help. Enlightening perhaps, but nowhere do they tell you how to make these double-barreled mixoscopic deviations a healthy and productive part of your personality. It is all get rid of, overcome them, when I want to integrate them, make them recognizably my own. Nude beaches, you say, but it is winter. Everyone's inside, wrapped up with a lover, the way I used to be with June. Havelock doesn't mention this. He doesn't talk much about loneliness, but makes several clinical points. The average exhibitionist is nearly thirty at the time of his first conviction. Rather revealing. Exhibitionists tend to be 1) insecure 2) drunks 3) mentally deficient. They love the "unusual, the remote, the exotic."

At four, regular as a machine, dressed in her slick, purple coat, she comes through the door. I watch through a hole in her iced window. The cold is particularly bitter this day and snow has crystallized on her hair. She should get a hat. We have an hour.

She is before me. She has a fine, lanky body, and those boyish characteristics I like—small breasts, small ass. Her hair is tintype brown and falls down to the nape of her neck. Ah, only this hour and the hour in the morning, and the dull, gray winter days between. She walks back and forth in front of the windows, reading, or perhaps reciting lines. I sit naked with the Globe. Before I was always clothed, with my eyes supposedly averted to the news. But now all pretense has been shed, like a molted skin, and I sit and watch, my eyes straight ahead. I drop the newspaper and walk about my livingroom, performing little duties, like stage business, all the time wanting to find the deep angst of a method actor. At the last minute, the last minute before he arrives home, she slips on her red bathrobe.

He comes in, kisses her. It is something I do remember. But suddenly he notices me, back in my favorite chair, naked, except for the want-ads. He moves directly to the windows and brings down the left shade (my right). I take it as a symbolic statement, a signal across an unbridgeable river, not as a warning.

2

I felt bad that night. Caught red-handed. And I would like to be a good neighbor. I do not want to terrorize anyone with my nakedness. If forced to, I could go back to the Combat Zone. Pay for my pleasure, although my trust fund is not unlimited. There's a fair amount of contentment among the men who visit the "Live" shows in the Combat Zone. The men I see at live strip shows seem all too happy to sit and watch and be entertained, and not have to act. It's simple and clean. But most men who frequent porno films, or at least the kind of films shown in 25 cent booths, want to watch difilement and want to be defiled. And the movies are short! It takes more quarters than a washing machine to get the job done.

But I realized I had no desire to go back to The Zone. I didn't want to leave my apartment at all. I didn't want to watch naked women, I wanted to watch this naked woman. I began to wonder if she agreed with his decision to pull down one of the shades, to cut my vision in half, so that, for example, I couldn't watch her cook anymore. Oh, the fun I had had guessing what she was making!

I wouldn't know the answer until morning. If she was there in front of the window to watch me dress, I could assume that she wanted to continue, that she too found something unusual, remote and exotic in voyeurism. It was, however, sometimes difficult to tell if she was there watching at all. I'd turn on my desk lamp in the morning so she could see, but unless she walked near the windows I couldn't see her clearly in the unlit shadows of her apartment. Only the red glow of her cigarette told me she was there.

In the morning, a cold morning the color of ashes, a shadow moved to its usual spot and lit a cigarette, and I exulted in this small triumph over her small-minded boyfriend. Or was he her husband? It didn't matter, for our nakedness had triumphed, risen, as if from ashes. I'd come to love routine, or at least the twice daily routine of our strippings. I put on the best damned show that morning. It was like mastering a sport. All the fundamentals become integrated, practice and routine drive them into your psyche, until you can at last perform freely, with imagination. I had the fundamentals of dressing down pat. I took some imaginative poses!

Then, suddenly, I realized there were two figures in the shadows, and two lit cigarettes. He hadn't gone to work. He'd been watching the whole thing. Now he knew for sure. Not knowing what to do, thinking slowly like a captive animal, I switched off my light, and hid in the corner. And waited, wondering if they were laughing at me, and hoping they were arguing. The river swirled before me like a Van Gogh. The window face, divided by a plank nose, looked at me, one eyelid drawn down in an exaggerated wink. I fixed a vodka and grapefruit juice, crying.

As I watched those two in the shadows, I thought of June. Now that he knew, for sure, would I ever see her dress and undress again, or even watch her cook. I thought, suddenly, of going to her, intercepting her at the door at five till four, talking to her straight about our problems. But I didn't go to her. I started to write a letter. I wondered if she would show it to her husband. Was he her husband? Was June my wife? Was she June? Am I Rumpelstiltskin?

But it was hard to be alone. Not only her husband was there, but other neighbors could possibly see in. I know this worried her and I understood how she felt. The city thwarts every attempt to be alone and naked with your neighbor. The challenge, as Tolstoy said, is to come face to face with life, and everywhere there's interference. Interference from husbands, neighbors, parents, the fact that we choose to live in separate apartments! And worse, my conscience. This banal, evil lobe in the deep six of the brain which prevents life at every turn.

For though she performed for me this afternoon, as usual, and stood in front of the refrigerator light like a goddess, leaving her bathrobe open so I could see the black V of her pubic hair as she moved with terrible grace from room to room, when he arrived the spell was broken and left in shards. Not brave enough to close the other shade while I was watching, he closed it during the night. Probably went into the room at two in the morning, knowing that such a heinous crime deserves not the daylight. I awoke this morning, ready to strip, only to find horrible white eyelids drawn down, leaving me no window upon my soul except my own.

The days grow longer and my voice deadens. My thesis is not going well, though with her windows closed I am not easily distracted. Yet, I languish. I enjoy my suffering. Once, figures or shadows of figures played across the screen of her livingroom. And I was all audience. It was a play, unscripted, with silent figures moving through golden theatrical light. But now it's blank. Just shades and curtains! One by one the windows close. One by one my neighbors turn their backs on me. They've had a meeting. The men got together and decided my nakedness was assaulting their women, and the women assented.

It was all like this for me. For a while I came to accept it. I began to meditate upon the blankness. But the object remained, and the questions wouldn't stop. I maintain a certain fondness for them. Did she want it this way? Did she grow bored or tired? Had I frightened her? Or isn't it just like a woman to cut things off just when they move beyond common morality. And then there was him. Perhaps he had insisted and she was but a slave to his desires. I've never liked him much. I can't believe she's quite satisfied with him. I can't believe she doesn't want to see me one more time. Give me one more chance.

3

But I waited and the chance didn't come. Only occasionally, late at night, would I see her face appear from around the blinds. So my life grew rather dull, even the idea of going outside, even in daytime, began to grow on me, like new skin. And I thought about it: what might I find out there in the stream?

I was afraid I would only find my old self, dispersed in the sickening effluvia of mankind. Better to stay inside. But then, it was getting a little boring and deadening. I could go see a matinee! There is something quite wonderful, I was telling myself, about enjoying an afternoon movie—long as it wasn't too dirty. I didn't want to sit among the masturbators. Perhaps I would go to see an adventure movie.

And I did, at last, go out, though not to the movies. I simply walked. It was quite a nice thing walking, trying out one's motor skills, "afoot with my vision."

Of course I had a certain fear of running into June. And worse, of talking about our theses. She'd probably be done with hers, and finished with Harvard. She could have moved out of town, I didn't know. She could have married without my knowledge. All this depressed me, so I drank. Do you know the Plough and The Stars on University? Thirtyish hippies, and poets, and some neighborhood people.

I did this, this drinking, and then I walked some more. And I was happy. Until I met her at the bookstore. Or really before the bookstore. Actually, I followed her there, though I too was headed there originally. It was 4 p.m. Time for her to come home, although I'd lost track of her comings and goings. The shades prevented all. So I was surprised to find her on Harvard Ave. at that time of day walking before me, her small ass in tight orange pants like the face of the moon. I hurried forward and walked but six paces behind her. It had been so long since I'd actually seen her. I suspected she was going to the bookstore; I'd often seen her walking about the apartment with an open book, reciting lines. Poetry? Drama? I could give her my thesis to read. If only I'd carried it with me. Everything would be explained!

We entered the store almost simultaneously. I walked to philosophy, she to drama. And so it was true. She was an actress. It was too good to be true. She was smaller and less angular in person, or rather, close up. Her face was nice. Her nose lacked a bridge and that, along with her seal black hair, made her look Chinese. Fortunately I was quite drunk by this time.

I returned Nietzsche to the shelf and moved toward her. She read Eugene O'Neill. She appeared quite absorbed in the book and I hated to interrupt her. But my head swirled with desire. I needed her. The fluorescent light of the store swam through the aisle like eels. Blue veins in my hands shone like twilight on the desert. It was very beautiful.

"Come home," I said quietly in her ear. She didn't recognize me though. "Don't you see, it is not too late. Come home, June."

"I'm not June. Who's June?" she said. And then, "Leave me alone. Who are you? I'll call my husband."

"Your husband?"

"He's the manager of this bookstore. Leave me alone."

"The manager? My God. Don't you know me?"

She looked down the aisles. She dropped Eugene O'Neill on the tile floor, and walked toward the back of the store. It was beautiful the way she walked. Wait, I said quietly, and followed her. She turned to look back and I opened my coat. She stopped for a second as if she'd begun to understand who I was. I unbuckled my jeans and pulled down my pants and underpants. I couldn't tell her response; her face was Chinese.

But suddenly he was behind her. And then beside her, his expression clear. He must defend her. "Come home," I said once more, flogging this person I am. Things were stock still. We saw each other at right angles. Nothing flowed and nothing happened, as always.

I pulled up my pants and walked home. I didn't care what they did any longer. They could call the cops or fuck in front of the window. I enjoyed the walk home despite the cold. I felt delirious, relieved.

Today, like all days since then, I did not wear clothes in my apartment. I did not dress and undress. I worked steadily on my thesis. At four, the usual time, I sat in my favorite chair and read the Globe. I couldn't see her anymore, though perhaps she could still see me, fisherman without a line. It was all like this for me, until, miraculously, like a gift of light, a new window opened.

The Learys

MANDY LEARY, THE girl next door, Big Mike first saw in the local *Willy Wonka and the Chocolate Factory*, this some time before he and his family had moved in, his Ally also in that show, the "ensemble." Mandy was featured, playing the part of a stylish but spoiled bitchy little girl whose father pampers her, the name of the character on the tip of his tongue. The Leary apartment abutted his, the little ones often out front in the driveway playing, yelling, running around, Branden included. He was fifth grade back then, like Ally, but didn't like school, and had that green hair. They were six, the Learys. One day Mike had dropped Ally off and there on the sidewalk across from Richmond Elementary were Branden and Dierdre and she was dragging him and saying You're going to school but he was screaming You're hurting me, you're killing me, his shirt half way over his head like a dog had him. Dierdre wasn't really hurting him, of course—we've known her for years—and everybody has to go to school, but Mike says he was to later understand, from Ally, that Branden after that was home schooled. At least for a time.

I'd known Mike for a long time, but I hadn't rented to him before then (it was kind of surprising he'd never got enough money together to buy a house in El Camino back when houses were affordable). It's a decent apartment, if a bit tricky, the complex walls so thick he doesn't hear his neighbors even when they take a shower or flush the toilet, had never heard an argument. (I wish all my complexes were built that good.) His door is on the second floor, the first floor being for parking, and there's a third floor—it's rather complicated, like a 3-D jigsaw puzzle, the Leary's was, #3, a half floor up from Mike's, just as #4 appears to be a half floor above #3.

Mandy's lover had also been in the ensemble. Big Mike didn't know her name, but perhaps Ally had kept the playbill, yet there were a bunch of girls in the ensemble. She had stood out though. She was about a foot taller and thirty pounds heavier than the other kids and looked awkward dancing in the show, but anyone who wants to participate in a Rec production is given an opportunity. The girl is Mandy's age, ten back then, eighth graders now. She's nearly six feet, dwarfing Mandy whose scarcely got any bigger and is like a doll really with that pale Irish skin of hers and those freckles on her back. But the girlfriend had slimmed down since the play, her hair black, cut short—mostly she wears black—and she wasn't unattractive, Mandy obviously thinking not. Yet if you were to see the girl, you'd have to say there was something different there. We all know that in Ally's grade there is a girl who is a biological boy (Dominic) who now is a girl (Dominique) and dresses for school likewise. What can you say? Mike says he feels like he is watching something he's not part of.

The girls liked to hide on the steps between the Leary door and the one above, after school when the rest of the family was absent. Returning home, Mike would sometimes find them there on the steps, talking, hugging, going to town, or he would hear them, though not see them, from his bedroom window when it was open. (Soon after moving in, Mike had moved solo into one of the two bedrooms in their apartment, as Ally got scared at night, Cynthia snored, and anyway he wanted his own space and says the noise from LAX—where he works—doesn't bother him. Our town abuts the airport. You grow used to the noise pretty quickly, just ask newcomers. The jetliners slowly emerge from the trees, in a kind of regal manner, before they head out over the ocean.)

His room was, at the time, next to Mandy's, though she shared a bedroom, no doubt one reason she was often about, mostly at Rec Park, which is in a swale in the middle of town, off Eucalyptus. It's well known around here that Big Mike, weather permitting, takes his constitutional each evening in the park, and that's where first, walking up the incline near the softball field, he espied Mandy with the girl. The big girl's back was up against the trunk of a one those damaging ficus trees—we're tearing them out on Richmond—Mandy meanwhile seemingly entreating her in the way a lover does when there's been a disagreement. As for Mandy, her back was to Mike so he couldn't be sure what it was he was seeing, but the two girls were standing so abnormally close to each other his suspicions, if not hackles, were raised. Middle school girls are often half in love with each other, we know that, but this looked different, fantastical, he said–especially so in that sunset, a baby blue except for the clouds, which had taken the pink coloring. Another time the girls were walking down Grand Avenue coming from school, their hands entwined. Long Beach and of course West LA are meccas for lesbians, but we rarely see lesbian couples in our town. Come to think of it, PDA's of any kind are rare here west of Sepulveda. (Or barking dogs, of any kind, come to think of that.)

Mike saying to his wife, upon return to his house: Mandy had such a beautiful voice and was so girlish in the play.

So you're in love with her, Cynthia joked, then reminded him of the case of lice that had swept through that production. They'd got an email home saying check for lice and sure enough Ally had it. It was a product of sharing wigs (girls in any case more prone to lice than boys).

Around the time of the school incident Mandy had run away from home. Why Ally had that info Mike couldn't say. Mandy plays "the girl" in the relationship apparently. The boys in her school must consider it a waste of talent, but Mike's concern is the parents primarily. Mandy's father drove a black Ford truck and worked some kind of manual labor job (he's a nice guy: when Tony learned that Ally walked to school in the rain on days Mike was gone to work, he suggested she could ride with them). It must be tough on him in particular, embarrassing, Mike felt–although as for that, it's usually the mothers who give their daughters the most grief.

Ally was only ten at the time and Big Mike didn't want her exposed to Mandy's shenanigans. When Dierdre would come home with the little ones, the big girl would bolt right past his window–one time he was naked–then down the back steps. She'd return a short time later sometimes, so he figured she lived nearby (he'd scarcely stopped to think about what her life was like, what she went through at school and with her parents, or parent, and everything).

They'd run into the Learys, including Mandy, Easter last at St. Anthony's, otherwise he wouldn't have known they were Catholic (which Cynthia and Ally are)–although you might guess so from a name like Leary. Mandy was dressed in her Sunday best, and Mike claims you would never have guessed she was any different than the other young ladies. After genuflecting, the Learys sat down right in front of Mike and his family, comically from tallest to shortest. Mandy, her brown hair the same color as the pew, was third from the left; then came Branden, followed by the two little sisters. Some one of them was wearing perfume. Do most lesbian girls wear perfume, who knows? In any case, the scent mixed with the incense, no doubt a special Christmas incense.

During the service Mike found himself recalling a time in college when he'd briefly dated a Catholic girl, a high school student—he was already once-divorced and had a child—and he went to a Catholic priest to discuss matters, because when the girl found out his marital status she said she no longer wanted to see him. "I don't believe in, if it feels good do it," he'd recalled her having said at some point earlier. The priest's only response was to say that we are either going to follow God's teachings or not. That had taken Mike aback (he was as a lapsed Brethren at that time), and recalling it now gave him even further pause, especially since he'd wound up with a Catholic girl after all.

Midway in the service that morning the priest asked the children to come forward, and all but Mandy among the Leary children did. The kids sat down quietly, cross-legged on the step in front of the altar, Ally next to Branden, the priest telling the story of the Resurrection and in the end each child was to take a tiny cross home with them.

One day Big Mike's hand was forced, so to speak. He was reading our local rag, The Breeze, when he heard a knock on the door, only to find of all people Branden, come to ask Ally to play. One might guess that home-schooling was giving the boy cabin fever or something.

Hi, Mr. Reems, Branden spoke up—his face gentle, the smile a bit impish, according to Mike.

He was surprised by the "Mr. Reems." Everybody in town uses "Big Mike."

Maybe it was the green hair and what he'd seen at the school, but Mike says he hesitated there for a moment, Branden waiting on the doorstep like a foundling. More than once Mike had encountered him (garbage still a man's job) at the dumpster, which serves all five units, and on one occasion had had to remind Branden not to toss the bags of garbage into recycling whereupon Branden offered up that quiet, almost dangerous smile of his and an okay.

Hold on, Mike was now telling him there in the doorway, I'll go upstairs and check.

Ally was asleep, Mike returning to find, unaccountably, both Branden and Mandy inside the house, and the door closed. She'd come to fetch Branden.

We didn't know where he was, Mandy explained. Mom sent me.

Mike hadn't had a really good look at Mandy, at her face, for a while—she'd been dolled up for the play, those years ago. Now she wore just torn jeans, a t-shirt, and tennis shoes; her hair was cut short but not cropped. Her roundish face was not, he felt, as elegant as he recalled. He didn't think "impish"—cause she looked pretty frightened—but "waifish," yes, he did think.

Go home, Branden, Mandy said somewhat harshly, or nervously maybe, when Mike reported Ally's condition. Mom says you still have your math to do, she continued.

Maybe Branden was on to her, who knows.

In any case, Branden was quick to the door, Mike catching the door right before it closed, not wanting to be shut in with Mandy alone. But the girl had apparently seen an opening and just sort of let herself down to the floor, like she was wilting, or chilling, whereupon she crossed her legs yoga-style (no doubt she, like most young actors, had had dance training).

My parents, they have the legal right, she began—looking up, talking to Mike like they were old friends—to keep me from my girlfriend? Is that true? Is it, Mr. Reems? I totally love her, you know.

She and Branden knew his name from his job on the city council perhaps. Or just the mailbox.

Maybe the big girl's name was LeAnn: Cynthia had found a torn–off piece of a note (on romantic bluish-gray paper) one afternoon next to the mailbox and passed it on to Mike. "Dear LeAnn," it read, "I love you so much and it...me to see...with." Like a fragment from Sappho.

I'm sure you do, Mandy, Mike began (he'd never addressed her before), but I don't think love figures in the equation.

Mike says he was stalling, in addition to trying to calm her, reassure her (but she wasn't crying).

He didn't say to her, and in any case I'm not a lawyer Mike jokes, that it was his impression that parents can determine their children's associates, even on a basis of gender- orientation, if they so choose. Mike continued to speak measuredly—just the way he is wont to do on the city council—because he wanted Mandy to know that whatever disapproval he felt it didn't extend all the way to general condemnation by any means. He also didn't want her doing anything rash again like running away. Mike had inquired with the police about her having run away and learned she'd stayed at the girlfriend's house, only returning home after some tense negotiations with Captain Rinaldi.

It's not my place to discuss these things with you anyway, I'm afraid, Mandy, he was to add. Have you spoken to a counselor, or a....

Mike choked on the word "priest," he says. That too a joke.

But my parents are going to kill me, Mandy said loudly.

That was when he closed the door. He had—and has—a public image to maintain.

Did she still do theater? Mike was thinking that her parents must have been so proud of her at Willy. Wasn't she their beautiful, talented first child, first daughter? Certainly she held a special place in their heart.

Maybe the thing she had for the big girl was a bit of theater, too, middle school theater, whatever else it was, he was also thinking. Or maybe a substitute for theater (acting, people find out pretty fast, is a tough nut to crack).

Again, Mike knew her parents weren't really going to "kill her" or physically punish her in any way, that it was just a manner of speaking (or so he at least assumed), but feelings about sex and gender and family run very, very deep, as we know, and he was sure her parents were probably at their wit's end, however accepting they tried to be. There were the other kids to think of, too. (Many who say when questioned on an abstract level that they would be accepting are surprised by their reaction when the unwanted virus comes to their own home.)

And ours is a small town even if we're near a big city.

He'd wanted to ask Mandy while he had her there, What do you mean by "love her"? Big Mike, a local boy, could remember his own adolescence, how strongly he'd felt things—although he'd never felt anything strongly toward a boy except rivalry.

He didn't get a chance that day to voice his question though. His Ally had appeared on the stairs. She was wearing just shorts and a lavender halter. She rubbed the sleep from her eyes.

Mandy? she said. Dad, what's up?

Mandy came to retrieve Branden, Mike says he explained.

Branden?

He wanted you to play.

Ally was confused but at last smiled, apparently happy to see Mandy. She'd admired her in Willy Wonka and had spoken of her on occasion and had herself the acting bug.

Mandy rose from the floor, with a certain amount of dignity.

Are you in Flat Stanley, Al? she asked.

Just ensemble, Ally confessed.

No doubt it hurt her to admit that. She had an average singing voice and that limited her opportunities in children's theater.

But Mike says when he looked at his daughter–she was perched half way down the stairs–he liked what he saw. She wasn't judgmental, was just her usual friendly, intelligent self.

That wasn't quite the end of things however.

There came another knock on the door. Cynthia, he was thinking? The big girl? Mike thought he'd seen her pass by the upstairs window earlier, provided it wasn't the leaf blower, but he assumed now that she wouldn't have the "balls" to come find Mandy at his place–but who knows, he also thought?

It was Branden again though. Mom says come now, happy to return the favor probably. Okay, Mandy said. Thanks, she said, before leaving.

Good luck.

Big Mike opened the door for her.

Ally looked at him querulously when Mandy had gone. What could he mean by "good luck"?

Not long after, the Learys found a bigger apartment across town, on Imperial. It cheaper over there because it's closer to the airport. Mike only occasionally sees the two girls now, most often down at the park, he says. Everybody's curious to see how it will play out next year at the high school.

Poison Words

I COULD NEVER quite ever shake the poison words. Somewhere in my vast, efficient salesman's mind–I'm not sure where–were those words which would snatch a sale from my wallet, my wife's wallet, and my baby daughter Christina's wallet.

Never say down payment but first payment. Oh how I longed to say down payment, to say drown payment.

"Well, Mary" (Mary was the hypothetical prospect and I the hypothetical John the Distributor, not John the Salesman, not John the Pots and Pans Man, pots clanging and dangling from my old wagon, say Eliza those sure are pretty flowers), say...

"Well, Mary, is that a new dress?" Always start with something nice, her hair, a picture on the wall, but be sincere, say...

"Well, Mary is that a new dress?" Would you like to take it off?

Always poison words, unspoken. Not sign this, but O.K. this, not lids, but covers, not sets, but groupings, not contract but agreement...

Then I drove home after driving all over the goddamn city, drove through quiet late-night streets, sweaty, stole home to the apartment, tie loosened, jacket off, jack it off, and more often than not with a Signed Contract and Sarah waiting for me, freshly showered...and I walked in and kissed her, dropped my comb, keys, watch and wallet fast on the dresser. The wallet always thudded louder than it should and it seemed like Sarah could tell. "You got a sale," she said.

I looked up slowly and she hated and loved me for this because it drew out the moment, made time hover in the space between us. I watched her wait. She looked so freshly showered, dressed in a cool blue shirt exposing her thighs, those unclad legs that used to kiss the hardwood gym floor.

"You got a sale, Jack? Come on."

"Yeah, got two," I said one hot June night. It was the first time I'd ever sold two sets in a single evening.

"How'd you sell'em?"

"Charm. I think they find me attractive, just like you, my dear," I said.

"Come on Jack, don't kid. I suppose they let you make love to them, just like me."

"Most aren't as good as you, but they give me a down payment," I responded.

Unamused, Sarah walked into the livingroom and turned on a late night talk show. I knew she was angry, but I let her sit for a while. I noticed once again her clean, easy movements, combing her hair with her hand, waiting for me to apologize. And I remembered that first time we'd made love, how on a roasting May afternoon we fled Phoenix and drove to northern Arizona. Sarah was a senior in high school, I was a junior. I was a basketball player, she the "head" cheerleader. Back then everyone wanted a Midwest cheerleader with a brain–Sarah was from Michigan, and was a good student.

We were glad for the rich greens and browns of the north, the rough-bark trees and wet pine needles. At her suggestion we repaired to the car, out of the chilly Flagstaff wind. Soon I was kissing her, and moving my hand slowly in circles on her skin. But when I slipped down from her breasts to between her legs, she stopped me; she shuddered underneath my hand.

"No, Jack, I'm afraid. You talk sometimes about having a lasting relationship just so, it seems, we don't have to have one," she said.

"Maybe," I responded, "but I don't like how you bring these things up just when I'm having these good feelings toward you. And when I feel, besides, like an overdue geyser and you could get me to promise almost anything."

"But you know you can get me to do most anything," Sarah said, and turned away from me.

"It is a shame, isn't it?" I joked, and relenting, she turned back. I slipped her pants to her knees and mine to my knees, knowing that this time she wouldn't stop me. She wanted me, and as any good American boy would I took advantage. Still, even then I knew she was right. I didn't want a permanent relationship. I didn't want a home. But in late summer, like magic, Sarah stopped bleeding. In cool, early November we married. And in June, Christina was born.

Sarah remained in the livingroom watching TV. I sat down beside her.

"I'm sorry, Sarah. Just kidding, you know, about the down payment," I said.

"I know, Jack, I know...you bastard. Lie down," she said.

She began to undress me. With some good work clean and easy then dirty and rough, me passive as a lamb, she made me rise up. And I thought to myself (rather miserably):

"Well, Mary, if you order your grouping tonight, you receive an extra special free gift, our deluxe mind waker. Wanker. I mean salad maker, of course."

Since Friday night was a bad selling night, Mr. Drummer, with forethought, scheduled our weekly meeting then. Our division, which ran from Phoenix to Tucson to San Diego to Los Angeles, was named the "Roadrunners." All of us Roadrunners would get together every Friday evening and tell our sales reports and how we sold'em and talk about the progress of the company and sing songs in order to create enthusiasm. Under Mr. Drummer's direction we'd begin each meeting with a medley of "Everyware" songs. Mr. Drummer, who'd been a cookware salesman for most of his adult life, was a good-looking man, tall and almost slim, with a smile that had helped to sell thousands of pots and pans.

First, there were the national songs. Drummer said he especially liked our version of "Clementine," because he used to sing it as a poor boy in Florida. Back then he sang the original.

We'd sing:

In the desert, in the mountains,
By the seashore's foggy brine,
Sell your Everyware here to everywhere,
For our salesman will rise and shine.

Wives were encouraged to come to the meetings so Sarah did and she sang, but, to her credit, she hated it. She was also unwilling to find a babysitter for

Christina so the three of us spent every Friday night singing together, although Christina sometimes cried or, usually, slept. After the sales reports the meeting was rounded off with our own "Roadrunner Division Song," to the tune of "Caissons Go Rolling Along." It closed the meeting in the same spirit in which the meeting had begun. It closed it as nicely as we closed sales.

> Over pots...beat the pans,
> Yes our Everyware stands
> As the symbol of our livelihood!
>
> For it's more money
> With Everyware for me
> Shout out for Roadrunners loud and strong! Beep! Beep!
>
> For you'll always know
> That we will still the show
> As the Roadrunners go selling along!

Then, in case we hadn't had enough, Mr. Drummer and his wife would invite all the Roadrunners and their wives over to their house. The after-meeting parties consisted of more Everyware talk and a lot of drinking. I never talked Everyware, a language of little interest and great detail, but sometimes I drank a great deal. Often I drank a great deal.

But I didn't go just to drink. Sarah never wanted to go, but would—she said Drummer was an ass and smiled like an alligator, which was absolutely true. I wanted to go to the parties, I suspect, because I wasn't ready to go home, to be again the young husband/father. Even further dues as John the Distributor was preferable. Even when we did go we'd leave pretty early, and have to wake up Christina, though the ride home would put her back to sleep. Sarah loved being home, taking care of our home, and me. She'd hold me tight and I'd hold her in my arms, she beneath me, and me pushing it into her again and again. Sometimes three times a night. Finally we'd roll over to separate sides of the bed, because I couldn't sleep if she was touching me—not Sarah but anyone. I also couldn't usually shake the Friday night fight songs, which had changed since high school. Those goddamn Everyware songs sang in my brain.

Over pots...beat the pans,
Yes our Everyware stands
As a cymbal of our livelihood.

Friday night would carry over to Saturday morning. I would often have Everyware connected dreams. I would even wake up with the songs still in my head. Then, at times, I'd also bring the late Friday drunk to early Saturday morning.

Saturday was a big selling day. Each day of the week except Sunday was a certain kind of Everyware day. Only on Sunday did I sleep late, and feel my body shape the bed, and take my time with the sports page, seeing just how many hits the Cleveland Indians got. I was born in Cleveland, raised in Indiana, but woke up that morning in Phoenix, Saturday morning. On Saturday you had the whole day to show the others what a good salesman you were, for you were working for yourself of course but also for the Division: "Because if everyone tries to beat each other than we all profit." I thought this was pure horseshit, but I needed the money and did enjoy outselling the others. So I made it morning breakfast at Sambo's.

Waking up to two-toned Sambo's, orange plastic cut into patterns of pink plastic, is like waking to some wild, worn-out vision of the future from years past. In Arizona, nothing is brighter than the sun, nothing has shade or tone so even Sambo's is washed out. I walked in late and sat down in one of their ripple-cushioned wrap-around booths with all the other Everyware men.

Mr. Drummer spoke. "Now that Jack has managed to get out of bed," then the alligator smile, "and go out into the world," again the smile, "I would like to pass out a newly recieved brochure from Everyware headquarters," pause, "in Columbus, Ohio." I could see the Everyware night angel beating across this U.S.A. earth to deliver our brochure, and I remember how it began.

For a happy, bright future plan ahead, get your cookware early,
before you're married, and even before you're engaged—be ready.

Let the truth be heard–every girl has visions of a dream house,
with that man in your life, living, loving, fucking and showing
your friends your furnishings which say Ours, Ours, Ours!

Then Drummer said. "The first one to their car wins breakfast next Saturday," and I finished last. I drove leisurely out to West Phoenix where the girls were more domestic and traditional. I knew what I did. I played on their expectations.

The black roads were roasting; the streets melted desire, stole ambition, created mirages. Saturday's unwon breakfast could have cooked on those streets. Amid all this heat, I thought, how I am expected to concentrate, to remember all the tips Mr. Drummer had passed on to us Roadrunners.

Mr. Drummer said when you first make a call, when you first knock on the door, you should be thinking: "The girl behind this door has $50 of mine." This $50 was the down payment. I arrived in West Phoenix, stopped at a large apartment complex. My eyes passed down the row of doors–and I couldn't help but wonder which girl had my down payment. I was scheduled to call on a young woman named Natalie Hayes, who was single like most of our prospects, and worked as a receptionist in a dental office. And I knew if I didn't find Natalie's door very quickly she might spend my $50 on cokes or records or new clothes, instead of on her cookware, her future tools. I started to walk rapidly around the complex, 1A, 1B, 1C, 2A, 2B, 2C, rows of apartments, one row upon another, not exactly dream homes, say...

"Well, Mary, you got my $50, hand it over."

Suddenly I stopped. I hadn't been looking for Natalie's apartment at all, I'd been dazzled by the complex itself, lost in the sheer sameness. Finally I did manage to think seriously about my Natalie Hayes, my PROSPECT, my receptionist, and before she knew it I'd been at her door, gone to my car to get her free gift, and returned with my suitcase, which was heavy and gray.

Natalie said, "You can come in and show me, but I can't buy anything."

I said, "Fine, I get paid for advertising Everyware, too," which was untrue.

Natalie was a pretty girl. Her hair was blond, though her eyebrows were brown. I imagined the rest of her hair brown. Her mouth stayed open quite naturally, as though she were sucking in her breath. I skipped over the intro-ductory say-something-nice and pulled out her free gift, our famous Everyware Juice-Savor Pie Pan. I presented it to Natalie, my fingers extended below as if it were the crown jewels. Natalie appeared happy to receive the pie pan–she wasn't ecstatic, just thoughtful. But then, after determining Natalie's qualifications (her job, whether or not she already had her cookware, i.e., her tools, etc.), I did some-thing I'd never done before. As I brought forth the one-quart saucepan, pulled the pan from the velvet cloth bag, I said, handing Natalie the protruding handle, "Shake hands with Everyware, Natalie. Notice its sleek, modern design, feel the heft, stroke the hard, heat-producing handle." And there and then, poison words unspoken become poison words spoken, released into the general atmosphere. It was too late to say "feel the fine heat-resistant handle." There was little to do but plunge happily ahead. Natalie looked up and smiled and waited patiently for me to correct my mistake, or go on, or perhaps she wanted me to repeat it–who knew? I don't doubt that she liked sex. I wore my wedding ring but could have been laid, anyway, times before. I had already noticed Natalie's tight body, her Levied crotch hiding all that brown hair. But all these Marys had begun to merge. I would see Natalie for 45 minutes, then see another, ask the same ques-tions and receive similar answers. And so many of them would buy, so many saved for me my $50.

It would have been awkward to correct myself, and I was afraid to repeat myself. I found myself saying other forbidden things.

"Well, Mary," I charged forward, "if I'm going to sell you this hear Everyware, I'd better go on to step two of our 10-point sales program."

Incredibly, Natalie just nodded. I'd ask her small questions in order to get her to start choosing. Which color do you like? Which grouping do you like? Have you ever read Death of a Salesman? Natalie said, yes, oh that one, I think we had to in high school, respectively, and then bought her pans; nervously but full of hope, she pressed the ball point pen to the paper, marking her name indelibly to our Everyware contract. I was not surprised. When she'd told me I could come in but that she couldn't buy anything, I knew she would, or at least wanted to.

I packed slowly. I could see by Natalie's eyes that she was a girl who wanted things. "When will my pans come, Jack?" she said, stalling as I stalled.

"They'll come in about three weeks, Natalie," I said. "I suppose I should go," I added, looking at her.

"Yes," she said, almost like a question. Women, I believed, liked me because I "looked innocent."

But I decided to go. Out of loyalty? Maybe. Yes, I couldn't quite shake that. I left Natalie's $50 richer; she had bought my goods. I left her, but not to make another call like I was supposed to, because I couldn't concentrate in heat. I went to the movies, a double-feature. It was cool inside. Finally, I drove home.

Sarah had dinner ready and waiting. Fried chicken, one of my favorites. I smelled the chicken as I came through the door, and unloaded comb, keys, watch and wallet. I could hear Sarah in the shower. Christina was asleep in her bed, her toes curled around the bars of the crib and her face hidden behind her left hand. It was difficult to imagine her late-night crying.

I began to undress. Strangely, the moment was suspended, fried chicken crackling, water rushing, poison words unspoken.

"Hi," I said, climbing in the shower.

"Hi, honey, how'd it go? Give you a down payment?"

"I did sell one."

"Good. Great," Sarah said, then kissed me. "Mr. Drummer called, and said that you didn't check in."

"I went to the movies after the sale. Two Bergman films. It was like sailing to another world."

"Two depressing foreign films, I imagine."

"The second was a romantic comedy of sorts," I said, but my explanation was not enough. Sarah frowned and began to stroke her wet hair, and then turned to lather. I watched her, her hair reminding me of that rainy night that she told me she had stopped bleeding and thought she was pregnant.

I hadn't even seen Sarah in the two months prior. It was a cold, drizzly November night. She found me in the football stands. Sarah wore a beautiful red sweater and a burgundy skirt. She had never looked better. And I remember that I'd never fucked so hard as we fucked the night Sarah, in her red sweater, told me she had stopped bleeding. The thought runs over and over in my mind, and I've always wondered if she knew all along we'd been making a baby, sweating and pumping our young hearts and asses out those Phoenix summer nights. I mean, in 1969, did everyone take the pill, did Sarah think about it? Why didn't we know things grow in a cunt, that it ain't just a sperm bank, a creamy abyss.

"Are you sure, Sarah," I said, "it's me?" What else to say; my mouth filled with soap opera. "Oh, Jesus," I said and we walked down the grandstands together, friends saying hi to Sarah, glad to see us back together. They didn't know, like I know now, that things that matter most go on on the inside.

"It's you," Sarah said, "though I'm not absolutely sure I'm pregnant."

We walked and huddled under the bleachers. We held each other; it felt good to hold her again. It had been a long two months apart. The rain made it seem longer. The rain made the hot Phoenix summer seem very distant—all was confused.

"Fuckin' cold, huh," I said, and then I kissed her and felt the warmth of her breasts and wanted to bury my head between them. Sarah started to cry. She cried a lot. Her tears froze on my cheeks, like the rain.

"Yeah, fuckin' cold," she said, managing a smile.

We walked to my car, leaving the football game, and then just began to drive. Once inside my Plymouth—actually my mom's Plymouth—the memories flooded in. The backseat of the car was the home ground of our growing child and soon to be the sourcespot of our marriage.

"I suppose there's nothing to do, huh?" I said rather vaguely, not knowing exactly what to do, stunned. I hadn't been planning on anything except the coming basketball season.

"Nothing but make love," Sarah said.

"Yeah sure, why not? We'll have twins." We both laughed a little.

"It could possibly cause a miscarriage," Sarah explained.

Sarah and I drove out to our favorite place on the Indian reservation, not far from our houses in Scottsdale. We pulled to a stop along the canal. I wanted to comfort her and tried, but I wasn't ready for a kid—although part of me always had been. I always expected marriage and children. It had been two months since I'd been laid, so with the moon full and shining upon her slim body, I slipped inside her and fucked as hard as I could, part of me wanting to rip her open, part wanting to give her all of myself. Only a slim part thinking about a miscarriage. It hadn't really sunk in—"A baby." I admit it, it's possible that Sarah got pregnant that night.

And oh how I gave it to her and how we screamed, first with her below me, and then above me and finally, like a train, I gave it to her from behind, cupping my hands around her tits, my knees inside her knees, kneeling, like praying. Sarah's parents had been Catholic but dropped it, my mother had been Catholic but buried it and we were Methodist, and it struck me as I pushed deeper inside Sarah, her long brown hair falling down behind her shoulders as she rose up on all fours, rose into that knee-bent prayerful position, me edging up tighter to her, it struck me that this was probably the only time either of us had kneeled like that before God. But it didn't seem like that was what the Christians had in mind, the position was all wrong, unmissionary. All was confused.

I stroked in and held it there.

"What will your father say?" I asked. Sarah attempted to turn her head around to me. "No, no," I said, and buried my head against the back of her neck. "If we look at each other we'll just start crying." Inside I thought, if I look at you I'll see my whole future. Sarah started to turn around anyway. I put my cock up her as far as I could. "Don't turn, Sarah, you'll twist the damn thing off." She laughed and relaxed. "And then how will you prove it's me," I added, as a joke.

Sarah sank down upon the car seat; I fell on top of her, still attached. She started to cry. "I would never force you, Jack... I would never..." She couldn't say more and started to sob, almost convulsively.

"I'm sorry, I was kidding. Now tell me what your father will say, and your mother?"

"They will want us to get married," she said. And I knew she was right. There was the old country in them. They had come from the Ukraine to Canada to Detroit to Phoenix. Her father and his brother had married her mother and her mother's sister, and they had all moved around together and they worked the family optical business together. I would be expected to do the right thing. "What do you want, Sarah?"

"I will have the baby either way."

"Yes," I answered, and then slipped back into myself. For a moment Sarah disappeared. I felt naked and alone, out there under the moon on the reservation. Her pregnancy was a poison in my system. "We'll wait until we're sure before deciding anything, all right?" Sarah nodded. It was too early to be a hero, I thought. For tonight I will remain the villain, and so I made love to her once more, my hands around her breasts...

...just as I did as she turned back to me in the shower to lather. I eased inside her, water falling down our backs. "I saved you something," I said, remembering Natalie. We dropped to our knees. Sarah leaned against the white porcelain tub and with so much left to say we came like times before. And all the while I was wondering how long it would be before poison words surfaced at home.

The following Friday evening Sarah, Christina and I arrived late to the meeting, about midway through "Give Me That Everyware Spirit" sung to the tune of "Give Me That Old Time Religion, It's Good Enough For Me."

I was a little nervous. I needed to come up with a story for the "How I Sold'Em" portion of the meeting. I had sold just one set during the week, to Natalie on Saturday. A poor week. A rotten week. I felt as though they were going to know I was lying about how I sold her–I thought at least Sarah would know. I recalled show and tell in elementary school. Some kids had amazing stories to tell, but somehow I would believe them and the teacher would believe them. Then I'd get up and tell a good whopper, because I couldn't tell what I'd really been doing, smoking, kissing Liz Woolery, playing with switchblades, so I'd make up a story. When I'd return to my desk the teacher would say, "Well, isn't that an interesting story, Johnny. You have a fine imagination."

Harry Meeks, the man who originally had trained me to sell Everyware, stood up and told us all how he had sold'em. He was blond and skinny and tried to be enthusiastic and Everyware- like. But Harry, standing up there, gestering, forcing an enthusiastic smile which was on its way to being an alligator smile, still looked like a little kid with melting ice cream cone stuck in his hand. His very fat wife, Marjorie, also hated Mr. Drummer, but she sat attentively in her yellow two-tone dress and wanted a baby and kept sending Harry out the door to make more calls.

Harry sat down. After a brief introduction from Drummer—"Here's Jack Severall, one of the leading college Everyware salesman in the nation!"—I got up. Although I'd just been proclaimed a leading college Everyware salesman in our large nation, all I could see was small square room where fifteen people huddled before me who'd stopped on Friday night to be enthusiastic for an hour. And so the words I resorted to were not those anyone expected.

"My only sale this week was to a girl named Natalie. No one ever gives the names of the prospects they sell—my sale was to Natalie. Natalie. It was an easy sale, she wanted to buy no matter what I said. Mr. Drummer's right, they want to buy. Natalie hardly listened to what I said. These girls, many of them, still believe in the horseshit dream of this pre-sweetened world. Many will buy if you just create the right aura, make them feel the need for the homelife dream. I became the man in this dream and know exactly what I'm doing. I wear my wedding ring. I'm not one of those boy hustlers just looking for a piece of ass. SIT DOWN, PLEASE, MR. DRUMMER, I intend to finish." He sat. " No, I'm serious and responsible, working my way..." I stopped my speech. There was silence and pitying looks and nervous smiles. Sarah looked on and I felt bad for her. Christina remained asleep. "It's all yours, Mr. Drummer," I said finally, and I walked toward Sarah.

Sarah, it appeared, wanted to mother me. Or perhaps she wanted me as lover, proud of my defiance, wiping away one alligator smile. Her sympathy and love, however, appeared to preclude the hope that she had understood the implications of my little speech. Or maybe she did, she wasn't dumb. Maybe she knew and still managed to hang on and care for me. And I wanted to be taken care of, to be a poor little boy, and I wanted her in her early Midwestern way, dreamy, dreamy, suspended in time.

As I gave Sarah the keys to the car, Drummer said, "You're fired, Jack." I saw that as he said this he was in some pain; it would be hard to give up my sales. After all, he did have a living to make, a family to support.

I wanted to be alone. I grabbed my basketball from the backseat of the car and I left. I walked to an outdoor court and shot some hopes beneath the fluorescent lights. And around me lights of various distances blurred more and more in the black, still night till it was me watching myself, shooting, alone at the center of the universe, all else grown black.

The lights went off on the court at eleven. I went home. Sarah was up and waiting and watching a late night talk show, wrong channel. She sat up near the tube and stroked her hair. I sat down behind her on the sofa. She didn't look around. I wanted to say I was sorry, but I didn't say it.

"Soon as I'm gone, Sarah, you switch channels," I said. "You like different shows."

Sarah, admirably, didn't defend herself. I went into the bedroom, unloaded my pockets, and lay down on the bed. Sarah came in. I wondered if the thud of the wallet set off some conditioned response in her. Anyway, she stood near the dresser and wound my watch, which had stopped again. She would wind it for me because her hands were smaller and could get a hold of the little sucker knob better than I.

As always, Sarah was clean and pretty. But that night, not surprisingly, she appeared uncharacteristically sad and forlorn. The moment hovered in the room—had I stung her at the meeting? She combed her hand though her hair. I kept thinking that no man hath love like a woman...

And I lay on my back on the bed and waited for her to cry out, the welt inside her mouth, won't you scream, Sarah, won't you? Yet she wouldn't speak. She merely sat down on the edge of the bed. Her hand rested on my stomach, then slipped inside my shirt. Her fingers were cold.

"Jack," she said, and I was glad for her voice, "I know what you meant about the TV shows. I'll never be an intellectual like you. I know that there are things you want to do in life. I just want to be part of it."

And so it was my turn to speak; time for poison words at home. But when the time came they didn't feel poisonous, although they hurt.

"We don't have enough, Sarah. It's too soon, we are too young. I can't settle so soon for a sense of responsibility and a warm lay, and some laughs, some worries. I want the world and you want a home," I said. Yes, my mouth filled with soap opera. Say...

Sarah looked sadder than I ever remembered. "Do you think I tell all?" she said. "You, Jack, don't know what you want?"

"I know what I don't want...I know what I want. I want to separate," I said, and walked into the living room. Sarah remained sitting on the corner of the bed, her body bent. Her slender face, always a bit reticent to reveal too much, now fully bared its sadness. I wondered if I had ever looked hard enough before. Her eyes, her interminably hopeful green eyes, looked right through me as I came back into the bedroom. Sarah waited for me to speak, but I had said all that I had to say. Those necessary words now felt inadequate, although no less necessary. It was time for arrangements.

"I want a separation. You can stay here or you can go to your parents," I said, and Sarah suddenly looked stricken. It was as though she hadn't heard me the first time. Sarah was hysterical. I tried to calm her but I couldn't. So, fleeing the apartment, I ran to a phone, and asked her father to come for her. When I returned to the apartment I found Sarah sitting in the rocking chair, holding Christina, who was crying. "Get out," Sarah screamed at me when I asked if they were all right. I got out.

I drove to a bar—feeling somber, scared, drained to the last sigh.

In court, months later, Sarah gained custody of Christina. I gained the car, and alimony and support payments. Sarah lied in court when she said I told her to go home when actually I told her she could either stay in the apartment or go home. Maybe a minor point, but she lied so cooly, like a salesman.

The Longest Day of Summer

ABE THOUGHT OF Margie as he loaded The Times on the back of the truck. He had been expecting the delivery since midnight; he had sat under the yellow parking lot lights waiting for the news to clear the wires. He couldn't believe anyone would buy a paper which didn't include Saturday's baseball scores, but the Sunday Times sold well up north. Transplanted New Yorkers filled those New England towns, and they sometimes longed for the city. The Globe was the only alternative, save local papers like The Springfield Union. Abe had to admit that The Times magazine section was one of the best in the communications industry, though the rest of the news was too crammed together and confusing.

Late Night Johnny played The Kinks new song, "Give The People What They Want," as Abe tossed the last bale. God, but he wanted to get on the road. The headline read: "Israelis Push Toward Beirut." Saturday's Daily News headline read: "Booze, Young Boys and Bagels: The Secret Life of Slain Dough Heiress."

Margie would be waiting at the other end. Even if she'd gone out with friends Saturday night after work, she'd be washed and ready for him, lightly clad in her rose-print negligee, waiting for what she jokingly called his "special delivery." In fact, Abe's dallying with Margie the week before had put his job in serious peril. And it was her fault, or what he called his "love" for her that was primarily at fault (Abe a man who dispensed fault wherever possible—quite against relative times). He hadn't made it to Hartford until daybreak and Northampton until 6:30. The morning sun gleamed on the cab of his truck, like the aura of Jesus himself, as he unloaded the bundles at the State Street Market, Lizotte's Tobacco Shop, and Imperial Bagel. A few customers were up and waiting for the delivery. It was Sunday; no one went to church. They needed The Times.

Abe felt that he understood what it meant to those people. Good news and the ritual. He, himself, preferred The Daily News, a secret he kept from his employers, although punctuality was all they asked. But he understood; if Abe couldn't get his hands on The News as soon as he finished his route, with a cup of coffee and a chocolate honeydip donut to go along with it, then all wasn't quite right in the world.

And now as he once more headed north out of the city, Abe thought about his world. He'd written home to his folks and sisters: "Things are fine here. I have secured employment." He had also secured an apartment, on East 98th, and had been given a truck to drive. A Toyota longbed. Margie completed the trinity.

She had begged him last week. "Stay a little longer, Abe. God, I have to have it once more, Abe. I never know if you'll ever be back."

"Do not say 'God,' please Margie. Not on Sunday. Not about sex. His judgment is swift."

Though Abe did not exactly believe in God the way he used to (a relative position he despised in himself), he did believe that certain things weren't done, certain words weren't coupled...and twice on Sunday? Recalling the song, he had to laugh. Margie had snuggled up to his thigh. Oh, how he hated those insatiable rural folks. Just like his relatives back in Kentuckiana. Screwing their brains out. Spilling their brains upon the soil. Rich soil, foolish people, Abe thought. Never sire a Kentucky Derby winner that way! Never leave home. Abe took particular pride in being the first of his kin to move to New York. Also the first one to graduate college (Western Kentucky, B.S., Communications).

Margie had never left the Connecticut River Valley. Born in Windsor Locks, she'd never been farther than Windsor, a few miles down the road. Her relatives dotted the valley like flies on a horsehide. And not too sophisticated. Before coming east Abe thought everyone on the far side of the Midwest was sophisticated. He thought of Harvard, Yale, etc., and big money. Abe, himself, had come to New York in search of fortune. "New York," his college professor had said, "is the center of the communications industry." Since Abe had supported himself through college, and in fact through high school, on a paper route, start-ing off a career in New York doing something he knew how to do was a smart move. Though Margie had her doubts.

"One of these days, Abe Snickers, you'll drive up this river valley, park that truck, and let the damn New York Times rot in the rain. The Times doesn't need you, but I do."

He had answered her. "The world's bigger than this valley, Marg. Besides, the paper must be delivered. I'd do that first." And he supposed he would. No romantic flights of fancy. Margie wasn't going anywhere. And yet, as headed out of Oz into the black night of the north, here and there a cluster of lights like a dog chain, he felt himself swept toward her. "You may not be cut out for the city," he said to himself. And out in the black fields, with the fat cows, Abe felt the universe slip in his window. "Perhaps your archetype is the farmer," he continued, outloud, to himself. "Or the circuit rider. One doesn't escape one's archetype except at a price."

Abe had come to realize that he talked to himself, both when he was in the city and outside of it. He needed someone to communicate his thoughts to—the two hours he spent with Margie each week weren't enough. He'd first met Margie at Charlie's Beafsteak, where she worked as a waitress. Wasn't that perfect, he thought, I go half way around the world to meet a waitress. Fortune was the devil herself. But Margie, oh Margie, was smooth and kind. When he put his face to her breasts he was transported. "Just like the Indiana dunes," he'd said to her.

"Here, Hoosier boy," she'd responded, "they're all yours."

But it had not all been good times. It had been an unusually wet June, which bothered Abe but left Margie downright sullen. At times he worried for her mental health. A couple of weeks earlier, for no apparent reason, the back of her neck had broken out in a rash. Her nervousness upset him; and the rash looked like scales on a red snapper.

Margie was not there when he arrived. He had brought her fresh, seasonal strawberries, but she wasn't there to try some. Furthermore, he didn't have time to waste. It was 3 a.m. He'd done Hartford and Northampton, but Springfield lay ahead. It was the longest day of the year, the one Daisy Buchanan always waited for but missed, Abe recalled. But longest day or not, he had to get going.

Several times he'd suggested that they spend Sunday evenings together, after he had finished his route, but Margie always said that she had to visit her parents on Sundays. Now he began to wonder what she really did on Sunday nights. He knew she occasionally went out with friends, including male friends, but she'd always been there when he arrived, and not only there but ready and willing, with coffee brewed. Damn, Abe thought, and then he said it outloud, even though it was Sunday: "Damn. It's only once a week. Last week she begged me to stay longer!"

Abe felt a little foolish sitting in her driveway like that talking to himself. He needed to be on his way, but he didn't want to go without seeing her. Perhaps something had happened to her. He turned off the car lights and thought. The river behind the house and the thick-leaved maple trees disappeared. Her house became an outline, and the perversity of their late night rendezvous suddenly fell upon him like the pitch-black itself. "How can I leave Margie here all alone during the week? And probably violate my archetype to boot?"

Abe issued a short, satirical laugh as he silently repeated this statement to himself. What did I call it before college? Destiny? No, Providence was what the church said, but that wasn't quite right. Perhaps my archetype did not truly exist before college. Abe snorted, thinking: the way some people didn't truly exist in God's eyes before they'd met Christ.

As for Margie, he must find her. Fifteen years on a paper route and never once did he fail to deliver. This, no doubt, is one of the turning points of my life, Abe thought. His Daily News horoscope had read: "Have fun in the a.m. Be open to encouragement of associates, but beware of evil omens in the p.m." But now it was a.m. again, the sun soon to rise upon another Sunday, and Abe didn't know Sunday's horoscope, on that longest day of summer.

Father's Day, his sister's 30th birthday, and the summer solstice fell simultaneously on the 21st. Already Abe could see a sliver of morning light run up the river like returning salmon. He had fallen asleep for an hour. There was little he could do in the dark. Margie would surely show. But she hadn't. His choice was now clear, imminent: either head for Springfield, or, as Margie had suggested, let the news rot. Abe thought about all the people rising from their beds, putting on the coffee, showering, then walking down to the corner store for The Times, and finding only

The Globe or The Union. A week's expectation, the sweet lolling in bed with coffee and the best of New York, gone with Abe's love affair. Abe felt no little responsibility, but he had a sense that Margie was not home for a good reason. He wanted to make sure she was safe. Also, he wanted to lie next to her, if only for a short while. His loins sent minute vibrations through him. He must wait for her return.

Just then, just as the sunrise began to filter across her backyard, Abe noticed Margie stepping up the riverbank, gingerly, and absolutely naked. Suddenly, looking quickly at her neighbors' house, she dashed across the yard and in the backdoor. Abe felt almost guilty, sitting the car, watching her embarrassment. And he couldn't imagine what was going on. It was as though she'd emerged from the river primordially.

Now, Abe thought, I know she's safe; and I still have time to make my rounds. Then he stopped himself. What are you thinking, Abe? Go find out what's happened. He had to admit that he wasn't sure he wanted to know. Margie's vulnerability, the picture of her naked and nervous scurrying across the yard, made him fear his love for her. But he knocked on the door. Margie answered, still naked. What? "What"s going on, Margie? Did you know it was me?" Margie's eyes were wide as tablespoons. "Come in, Abe, you'll catch your death."

He wiped his feet on the black, rubber mat and entered. The sky provided the only light in the house. "Aren't you cold, Marg?" he asked, but she didn't answer. In the yellow kitchen, she poured him coffee.

"Have some," she said. "Reheated but good. I kept it for you. I thought you'd never come. I waited and waited but you never came. How come you never came, Abe?"

"I was here at three. As usual. Are you all right? I mean, why don't you put some clothes on?"

He didn't know what was wrong with her, but he didn't think it was quite the time to broach the subject of her stark early morning return. "Come, Margie, let's lie in bed awhile," he said, and she followed him into the bedroom. He pulled off his clothes and they hugged. Margie, however, was strangely impassive and foreign. She rolled away, her flanks shining like golden apples.

"I gave myself away, Abe," she intoned, not looking at him. "I gave myself when you didn't come. I got out of work early; it was still daylight. I waited for you, I waited for hours. Then I went to the tavern to shoot pool."

Margie shuddered, apparently on the verge of crying.

"I was here at 3 a.m., honey. You got mixed up. Maybe the light threw you off. I can't judge that. But I forgive you. What do you mean, you gave yourself?"

"I couldn't go through with it and he beat me and..."

"That's all right. No need to tell me. It's not your fault. You're all right? Not physically...hurt?"

"When it wouldn't work, he took a stick."

"Oh God, don't tell me, Margie. I don't need to know! Some things shouldn't be said. As long as you're all right?"

"But you weren't there to keep me safe. To look after me. He was an ugly, repulsive man.

"I killed him."

Abe tore at Margie's shoulders and turned her to him. He yelled in her face: "Stop it. That's enough. If you want, I'll never leave again. But no more blasphemies. I'm listening. Just tell me the straight story."

Margie reached for his member. "You mean this one," she said, and laughed hysterically. Abe was about to shove her away when he noticed her bleeding hand. The blood stuck to his penis as though they'd screwed during her period.

"What'd you do to your hand?"

"I stabbed him with a steak knife," she said, and Abe shivered. For a moment he thought she wasn't making it all up, that she wasn't lying. Her eyes were strangely steady and clear. And now she was looking right at him.

"I didn't know you went to pool halls," he said to her, but she just kept looking at him like he was saying something foolish or irrelevant. "You swear you're telling my truth?" he said to her. "The whole unvarnished truth?"

She was. The story hit the newsstands on Monday, when the days had once again begun to shorten. The Daily News carried it on front page, as did The Springfield Union. The Globe ran it page one, section two, "Metro/Region," and The Times buried it, in one column, on page 80.

Abe was fired from his job. But he married Margie, who was acquitted. They still live in the Connecticut River Valley.

White Fiction

CESAR THOUGHT IT might be nice to go through the summer session without having to teach Shakespeare. Or to stick with just a couple of the sonnets. Shakespeare was difficult. Some people acted otherwise, but they weren't being straight. One did of course enjoy the plays–Cesar liked Romeo and Juliet and Hamlet–but teaching them called for knowledge, expertise, a broad background. And if he screwed up, if some student raised a question about the text Cesar couldn't answer or if there were a passage he couldn't explicate, the usual unsaids would billboard the room: "Affirmative Action Baby" the first.

Besides, he wasn't sure he liked drama. His cultural heritage was already drama enough. Melodrama. Posing. Recrimination. Tears–so many tears! And not just by the women but also the Good Soldier men. Sentimental, macho, passionate, distant. Libidinous, but in a ceremonial way.

What he liked–"What I like," Cesar said to himself as he took his daily constitution down to Larchmont, for coffee–was fiction. The novel. A man's life was not a drama, not a poem. Not even a short story. It was a novel. It was Protestant, though Cesar was not. It was–well, "It is white." Or at least, that's what he, like Borges, liked best, White Fiction. Greene, Bowles, Lawrence, Ford Madox Ford, Henry James. The Brontes. He had *Agnes Grey* in his coat pocket. Anne Bronte was the least of the three-writing sisters, but to be the least of the Brontes was yet to be someone special. "The novel the most splendid achievement in the history of the world."

Cesar lived alone so he talked to himself, especially when walking. His life was not a novel. It was a walk. It was a walk down to Larchmont on a breezy spring day, the leaves in the wind leaping up against the blue like salmon climbing a falls. It was waiting for the Girls of Marlborough to appear at three p.m. It was, also, pressing his shirt and pants MWF before classes. It was wine. It was waiting for his daughter to call.

He sat down at the back of the Starbucks—not so friggin' cold in the back—and set to composing his syllabus. Usually he liked to sit in the front by the window and watch the whites, and Asians, pass by, while he read. The only brown faces were behind the counter or were those of women pushing a white child or two in a pram. The Koreans usually showed up in the late afternoon or early evening. Whites and Asians were forming a new culture, separate from, in LA, blacks and Latinos. White and Asian cultures had in common the desire of Asians to imitate white culture—or, perhaps, any modern, advanced culture. Cesar didn't blame them. Money, status, education, all counted.

When school got tough his white and Asian students dug in as if for dear life. But the Latin or black ones—or too many—would disappear. One day there and then gone, like a wife, or like those Native American students he had in Arizona, Apache and Navaho, who would go back to the reservation for Indian days, and stay. Where do they go—the white trash, too—when the school experiment is finished? To an early marriage, one kid on each breast, to alcohol, Cesar believed. To also, he acknowledged, more fairly, long years which would stretch out before them with a plain beauty, among friends. But also enemies.

Ivan Gregorio Madrid loved Shakespeare, existentialism, Richard Rodriguez, Plato, Goya. He loved way too much.

"I like people with versatility," he'd told Cesar, but Cesar distrusted such self-fashioning.

He gave his students a choice of calling him Cesar or "Mr. Aguero." Ivan, though intimate in his approach to things, chose "Mr. Aguero." Ivan was that formal-yet-social, isolate-yet-outspoken type redolent of Cesar's upbringing in Phoenix. Cesar's only Hispanic colleague on the Brentwood faculty acted in a similar manner. He apparently thought people should listen to him just because he had opinions and liked to express them. No doubt he'd grown up in a family in which opinions were valued not because they were right necessarily but because they were spoken with conviction, dramatically. Opinions were performed. And you listened to a son simply because he was a male.

Ivan was in the remedial class, the one before English 1. The class was made up mostly of Latinos, especially women, and some blacks. There were a half dozen whites, but of those, four were international students. There was a girl from Japan.

The first night of class, having written his name on the board, Cesar had shyly looked over the group, exchanged a smile or two, and then waited, silently, for the clock to click six. Outside, it was already dark, the windows shiny like black and white photographs. By the time the semester ended, the class would begin in daylight, and warmth, but that was a ways off yet.

Rodriguez's Hunger of Memory was on the syllabus.

"I've already read Hunger of Memory and also Days of Obligation," Ivan spoke up. "Should I read Brown instead?"

Ivan sat in the middle, toward the front but not right up front. He smiled a kind of knowing smile—open, even affectionate, yet a little too confident. He was not a handsome boy. His teeth needed fixing. He was short, and he would someday be squat. His face was too soft, too round. His ears were a little big—like a teddy bear's. He was dressed chino casual, his shirt open at the neck. Pale colors. Whitmanesque, was one way of putting it.

"No," was Cesar's response to Ivan's question. Cesar didn't explain either, not even a mollifying "it's worth rereading." He'd been around long enough to know when a student was asking a real question and when he was seeking special attention or a kind of intimate engagement. Cesar, himself, was handsome. Quite often students, mostly women but occasionally a young man, would come on to him. But he didn't respond, didn't fuck them, very often anymore. Nor, as he got older, did so many of them come on to him for sex. They sought a mentor, or a father-figure.

Heather, for one, had accused him of misinterpreting her interest in him. She'd been raised Jehovah Witness, but her father, it so happened, was a cross-dresser. Her mother despised him, had divorced him because of his fetish. The girl, herself, had not known anything about her father's secret until he had shown up at her high school graduation dressed as a woman. It was a relatively small graduating class—the ceremony was both secular and sacred, as most everyone in town belonged to the same church. The graduates sat on the stage. She saw him, her father, standing in the back of the auditorium. It was, she wrote in one of her essays, the only way he could get into the exercises unnoticed.

She was wicked smart, if limited by a lack of exposure. She wanted, like most of the others, a mentor.

"That's sexual, too," Cesar had said to her, and then spent the next few days worrying about his job. The thought of losing his job made him physically ill–just as when his daughter didn't call, Cesar, after a week or so had gone by, would begin to feel ill. In the pit of his stomach, as they say. And around his rib cage and temples. Yet he realized in shedding his wife he had shed his daughter, too; and he had done so, he suspected, in order to have time for writing. He believed most writers needed to live alone, and to learn how to be alone. At the very least, they needed time.

Teaching was demanding–or at least, time-consuming. It consumed time. There wasn't a lot of time left over. But Cesar had not really gotten around to much writing. A writer is someone who produces, over a substantial period of time, a body of work.

Ivan was probably gay. He was, Cesar surmised, in transition, in the process of coming out–no easy thing, especially in Latin culture. Cesar wasn't interested in Ivan in that way though.

But for some reason he didn't fully understand, he offered to drive Ivan home after class one night. Ivan had stayed around to ask a question. Perhaps just the secretive, taboo nature of chauffeuring a student home was what appealed to Cesar.

He'd bought a new car (perhaps that too was a reason), a Ford Fusion. They were on Bundy Avenue headed south.

"Just keep going straight," Ivan said.

They drove past street light after street light, red and green flashing in the foggy darkness like the tail of a Chinese dragon.

Ivan had started talking. He could really talk, really give his opinions. He was talking about classes he'd taken at UCLA before transferring to Brentwood.

"Lots of smart people at UCLA," he said. "And they study hard. But they are the same people who, in high school, didn't branch out. Many of them are, underneath the hip clothes, nerds. I like people with versatility."

Cesar was struck by the fact that though he and Ivan were pretty much strangers Ivan nonetheless was pouring out his soul to him. Maybe it was the ethnic connection. How lonely this young man must be. To be smart, gay, yet not really well trained—taking remedial English!—how hard it must be for him. His mother was off to pursue, late in life, a career in nursing, so Ivan lived alone in an apartment. No mention was made of a father, or siblings. Just his mother.

Finally, they arrived, at a large, standard-looking complex. The front of the building was modern, mostly glass with a modern Italian-style facade. Ivan talked a blue streak—about education, violence in the Latin community, anti-intellectualism in America. Cesar wanted to leave, but, idling there, both of them still wearing their seat belts, he let Ivan ramble on.

"Would you like to come in for a drink?" Ivan suddenly interjected.

Cesar killed the engine.

"All right."

He joined Ivan in the kitchen, quickly downing a beer. They talked about Los Angeles.

"I've been here five years," Cesar said.

"Any children?"

"One. Back in Phoenix."

"An only child."

"Yes."

"You live in Brentwood, professor?

"Call me Cesar."

"Okay, only for tonight."

"No, Larchmont. Hancock Park. Or near it. My philosophy is to live in the cheap neighborhood right next to a nice neighborhood."

Ivan laughed.

"Help yourself to another."

But Cesar didn't trust himself. When a pause came in the conversation, he fled.

Ivan missed the next class. It was his second absence—the class met just once a week—so Cesar dropped him. The first night of the class, going over the syllabus, Cesar had warned the students: "I've learned recently that my reputation as the attendance Nazi now precedes me. If you haven't heard it, believe it anyway. You get one absence, one only."

Ivan showed up the following week and was informed of his dropped status. Cesar saw in Ivan's eyes the hurt and disbelief, but oddly, no self-loathing. Cesar said, perfunctorily, "I'm sorry." He was sick of coddling students, especially Latinos. His people, Cesar felt, were rarely quite in earnest. Rather it was some sort of continuous performance. The drama, the poetry of the thing. Cesar's own daughter had dropped out of high school. Ivan was just too undisciplined. "He'll never amount to anything."

Although Asians don't hug, they do hold hands. Even mother and grown daughter. Two Korean girls had come in for coffee, holding each other's hand in a friendly, unselfconscious way. They were maybe sixteen. They took a seat in the back near Cesar and opened their textbooks. They were Marlborough girls and wore the standard blue top and short khaki skirt–though immediately after school many of the girls made the skirt shorter by folding it up at the waist. Underneath the skirt their were plaid boxer-like shorts–a school rule, no doubt. The girl facing Cesar perched one foot on a chair rung. Their eyes met. It was like class. The pleasure of class was such occasional secret exchanges. And even better, the secret meeting there, in public, with some student who had tacitly acknowledged the situation.

"Are you giving a show?" the other girl suddenly said.

Cesar turned his eyes away from the showing-girl. He looked down at his tall Americano. He always ordered the same drink: two shots of espresso and hot water. It cost $1.75. He was often astonished to see people order coffee drinks– lattes, etc.–that cost over three dollars.

It was then that he rose from his seat and left the cafe. At his car, he dropped off his Lit textbook and the unfinished draft of his syllabus, and walked down the block to the neighborhood bookstore, Chevalier's. Cesar was feeling suddenly excited. For there, in the bookstore, the whole history of fiction was at his fingertips once again. So much more to read! He'd never even read Jane Austen. Or Richardson. Or Dos Passos.

"Hello, Dr. Aquero?" he heard someone say from behind the counter.

It was her.

"When did you starting working here?"

Small

GENE SAW BRUCE come through the ballroom doorway and immediately he thought of Barb. So did everyone else at the reunion. They were twins. "Where's Barb?" he overheard Smiley. "I don't know. Everyone's asking me that," Bruce said, a bit peeved it seemed. He looked pretty much the same, dapper, self-possessed, compact, small. In high school, he wrestled. Went to State. At 103 pounds. Gene couldn't remember if he won State. It was funny to think that Gene's best friend, Epstein, had wrestled at 127, or 133, and now weighed around two hundred and thirty. A successful lawyer in D.C., Epstein like Bruce had starved himself through much of high school. Except– and Gene had felt let down by it–Biafra Day, which Gene had organized. A day of complete fasting.

And about Barb? Bruce didn't know? How odd, thought Gene. In twenty years a lot can happen, of course: best friends, and even brothers and sisters, can go their separate ways. But twins? For so many years you're a twin, almost hermaphorditic, and then after high school you're on your own, no longer a twin–that must happen regularly and it must be even more startling for same sex twins, but to completely lose contact with your twin, Gene found that odd. He determined to press Bruce on the matter later in the evening.

The ballroom, in which they all were to have dinner first, was filling up. Gene had returned to live in Scottsdale after some fifteen years as a wandering scholar, but he had never before been to the Camelback Inn. It was pretty, nestled beneath the mountain, and was softlit throughout the gardens and alongside the pool and even at the base of the mountain, dramatically. The pool water was an attractive serpent green. The palm trees swayed across each other like lovers. Inside, the tables were beautifully done. The silver was bright and went well with the girls' formal dresses—though of course the girls were women now. The fact that The Camelback Inn was a haunt of the asshole Republican rich he would put aside at least for one evening.

There was a bit of an awkward moment when Duggan, a friend since grade school, asked Gene to sit with him at his table.

"Thanks, Kevin," Gene said, "but I'm sitting over here."

"Oh, with the brains," Kevin joked. "The student council."

"I'll talk to you later, for sure," Gene said.

Epstein, Gill, Byrd, Sarah James, Duchamp—brains of a certain political, literary sort. But one nice thing was that no one really cared about any of those pretensions or cliques anymore. Oh perhaps Kevin did, a little, since in high school he wasn't quite an "insider," and perhaps the insiders didn't have to care, but my God, Gene thought, how amazing that we are here at all twenty years later—then, he thought of the few listed "In Memoriam." Most everyone knew Phil Tabor had been killed, in an accident, in college. "He had everything," Epstein said. "Brains, looks, athletic ability. Everything." Tabor won a scholarship to BYU to play football. But when they wouldn't stop trying to convert him, he left—for Colorado. Could be alive today had he stayed on at BYU, Gene ruminated, as his dinner—fish—was placed before him. Fish and chicken were the choices. And white wine or red wine.

Barb was obviously alive—or probably so—but Bruce apparently didn't know where she was—on this night at least—or didn't want to be asked about her whereabouts.

Gene would speak to him later. They'd never been close, but in high school there'd been a certain acknowledgment of each other—in life, there are always those others, not quite central but important. In the meantime Gene would enjoy the evening. The chatter and drinking were steadily increasing. When the award came for the oldest child, Epstein forced Gene to stand up. Epstein had, generously, gotten Byrd and Duchamp to go in on crib. "Twenty years old," Gene said, his glass of red wine in his hand. His son, Michael, had turned twenty in April. Everyone applauded Gene, a late round of applause for his high school marriage. A fine irony. His son's mother, because a year older than Gene—a senior when he was a junior—wasn't at the reunion. She had her own twenty-year the year before, and probably didn't win the oldest child award. But no doubt she thought about Gene during the evening, remembering him playing basketball (she was the head cheerleader), recalling, perhaps, his shy yet secretly confident manner, as so evident in the smirk he couldn't hide, and remembering, of course, those sweet desert nights, that first summer, when, rum and coke in hand, they discovered each other's body, the moonlight pouring in the station wagon windows, like gold—or rum and coke. Perhaps she had also thought about Barb.

Somehow she had guessed something was up. Gene wondered, to this day, how she'd known where to find them—Barb and him—that night. After the fight that followed, after the discovery of the two of them together, Gene never mentioned Barb's name again. Of course the marriage only lasted a year. Gene married so as to have rights to his child—a largely mistaken hope. When the divorce came he was stripped of nearly all rights, all contact. Those motherfucking lawyers and judges didn't know the first thing about the importance of men in children's lives. Or it was the party line. Or what was it they were thinking back then?

As one might expect, the head cheerleader had a sweet, small body. But not as small as Barb's. Seeing Bruce again, Gene realized why everyone so associated the two of them, Bruce and Barb. It was not only because they were twins, it was also because they were so small. Almost midgets, twin midgets. Yet beautifully proportional, like beautiful children. Bruce was maybe 5'1". He must have hated that in high school. He was popular, but still to be only 5'1" must have been a real drag for a boy. Gene himself was only 5'1" when he entered high school. 5'1" and wanting to play basketball. He was lightning quick and a deft ballhandler, but at 5'1" his chances were slim. He might, like Bruce and Epstein, have to turn to wrestling—a rather smelly, sweaty sport, to his mind. But then, at last, between his freshman and sophomore years, he got a growth spurt. Six inches. By his junior year he was 5'11.

Barb must have been 4'10, tops. She had the same build as Bruce, compact, sleek. Had Gene not seen Bruce, he might have spent the evening reminiscing about his son's mother's sweet body, and about how during sex she always came just seconds before he did—but Gene had got a bit caught up in the mystery of Barb, whose body he had only known once. And moreover, known it as it was then, twenty years before. Barb had not grown older. She would always be, for Gene, seventeen, but really, because of her small size, she would always be something like fourteen. And perfect. Naked in the backseat of the car. Her skin like light. Always—unless of course she showed up at the reunion and that didn't appear likely, which was nevertheless disappointing.

Still, Gene was having a good time. He and a few friends had drifted out to the firepit by the pool. Some people were inside dancing to the rock band, but Gene wanted to drink some more and talk with his friends, and maybe dance later on. The flames were beautiful against the charred black and ash white of the mesquite logs. The faces around him, flickering in the light, were familiar and yet not. Epstein, of course, he had seen over the years. He had seen the changes. But the others he had seen rarely or not at all. It was like claymation, computer graphics—the faces remolded or remodeled. The name tags were helpful. Bruce was among the least changed actually, Gene realized. "I'd better go see if I can find him."

"Be back in a few minutes," Gene said to Epstein.

"Don't get lost in the past," Epstein joked.

Ah, the past, yes. What a strange thing it was: it both existed and didn't exist. It was based on earlier experiences but wasn't those exact experiences.

His son's mother had not caught them in the car, thank god. She discovered them at the indoor skating rink, having followed them there. They were just skating, but they were holding hands. Gene remembered the sweater Barb wore— a mercury gray—and the feel of her cold hand. And then, when they came around the circle Gene had seen his son's mother, pregnant with his son, standing there at the railing, crying. She wore a fringed coat. She looked strangely beautiful to Gene at that moment. He'd run out, in his skates, to the Tower Plaza parking lot, but she was gone. Home? Even though they were married they were keeping up appearances by continuing to live at their respective parents' home. She was in college but still lived at home. Gene did spend some nights, especially weekend nights, at her parents' house. Not that night. He fucked Barb that night, after skating. Thank god she didn't get pregnant, too. She was a wonderful fuck. Gene could still recall it. He remembered slowly working it into her. His son's mother was a wonderful fuck, too. Gymnastic, as one might expect from a cheerleader. They were both wonderful.

Bruce, Gene was informed, had left. "He left with Tina Hirsch," said Mathers, winking. Maybe he'll show tomorrow at the barbecue, Gene thought to himself. Maybe even Barb will. Though that seemed doubtful, unlikely. Anyway, his reunion wouldn't come around again for five or ten years, so he might as well enjoy it. Gene finished the night off dancing, with Susie Barstow. He'd barely known her in high school. She was tall (and Republican?) but pretty foxy.

Susie and Gene had few common high school friends so they'd talked mostly about the present, about her job—she was a nurse in San Antonio—and about his son, which of course led them back, to some degree, to high school days.

"I remember when the rumor began to spread," she said. They were in her Camelback Inn room. The white curtains were just beginning to lighten as the sun came up.

Gene kissed one nipple, then the other one. "That was a long time ago, wasn't it," he said. "I always had my eye on you," she said.

He kissed her belly, kept his lips there. She'd never had children, she'd said. Perhaps she couldn't. Gene didn't know and of course he couldn't ask her. He himself didn't want more children, if he could help it.

"I thought Epstein was arrogant back then," she said.

"He changed after losing for Student Body President. But I always liked him." Epstein. Gene had known Epstein forever.

He worked for an Alaskan senator. He was the most successful of what Gene considered the "four"—himself, Epstein, Byrd, and Duchamp. Yet you could make the case that Epstein was the worst of the four since he switched from Democrat to Republican, was now a Reaganite. But he was hard-working, a good father—and a solid friend. You could also make the case for—or against, as it were—Byrd, since he had so many advantages—wealth, high intelligence, brawn (he played defensive end in high school), and was a first son. But maybe the pressure on first sons is sometimes too great, something Gene as a neglected second son was perhaps slow to recognize. Byrd wounding up working on the docks in Milwaukee, while supporting socialist's causes. He'd perhaps taken Lennon's "a working-class hero is something to be" too literally. All four of them had been in the Political Science Club, Duchamp the president. You could make the case that Duchamp was the worst–he was certainly the least successful and had become a libertarian and a gigolo. But Gene thought he himself was perhaps the worst.

At the barbecue, he and Susie returned to their separate group of friends. But occasionally she would look over at him and smile, and he would smile back. He would smirk, as, across the picnic tables and below the ramada balloons, the two of them silently recalled their night together. Gene had fucked her twice. The first time he came right inside her, like a husband. But the second time he pulled out and came on her butt. She had burned thoughts of Barb right out of him. Though now, at the picnic, he was thinking of Barb and Bruce again. Those two tiny twins. He was curious. Had they really lost touch? Even at Christmastime, they didn't get together? Amazing.

Then Gene saw Barb. She was standing next to the table with potato salad and green salad. She appeared, at that distance, virtually unchanged. Slim, short, fine–yes, Bruce's twin. Uncomfortably, Gene suddenly thought about overhearing his mother say one day, "I know someone like that. He's a time-bomb," and he had, for a moment, imagined his mother might be referring to him. Gene had wanted to say, "I'm not a time-bomb, Mom. Ticking. I'm alright, really." But of course his mother wasn't talking about him. Yet, now, seeing Barb again–but maybe it wasn't her. Gene had never really known her that well–a year or two of flirting in the hallways and at football games, one night together, one fuck, that was it.

But then Gene saw Bruce, right next to Barb. Of course it was her. So small, so seeming young.

Gene broke away from Epstein and Byrd and walked over to the next ramada to say hello.

He was sweating bullets. He felt way more shy than confident now. But excited, too. Gene was excited. The night before, with Susie, he'd been plenty excited, but this now was a different excitement, mixing memory and desire. A little voice in Gene's head said, "Holy shit, it's Barb." And Gene excitedly noticed how the late afternoon sun seemed almost to choose the next ramada, backlighting the scene like a sea wall.

But, when he was about ten paces away, Gene saw that it wasn't Barb.

"Hey, Geno," Bruce said, genuinely. "Man, you've hardly changed. Still in basketball shape, looks like."

"Thanks, but I'll tell you I sure don't feel the same," Gene joked.

"Like you to meet my daughter, Gene," Bruce said. "Barbie."

They shook hands. She was a lovely girl. A brunette, compact, dressed in a tank top and shorts. She looked at Gene straight on, without guile. He recognized an innocence.

"Named after your aunt, are you?" he said.

"And my grandma," she responded.

Gene looked at Bruce. He wanted to ask but now thought better of it.

"Your father was a heck of a wrestler," Gene offered, a bit weakly. "Went to State."

"He never told me."

"Well, he should have. I'm very glad to have met you, Barbie. Take care of the old man."

"I will," she said, and smiled.

"See you later, you two."

Gene turned to go. There were a lot of people to touch bases with—everyone understood that most conversations would be rather brief and light. And Gene was on guard. But when he turned to look back for one last look, he saw that Barbie was standing alone. She was picking at the carrots and celery dish. Bruce was talking to Smiley and Mike Woods, the class valedictorian (Woods was one smart motherfucker). Gene walked quickly back, hoping Bruce wouldn't see him approach his daughter. But just as Gene said, "Excuse me, Barbie," Bruce glanced over. A thrill ran through Gene, a kind of adolescent thrill.

"I meant to ask you about your aunt," Gene said—the word "aunt" almost sticking in his throat. He'd never be able to think of Barb as old enough to be someone's aunt.

Barbie brushed back her brown hair. She turned sideways to him. Her lips were bright in the receding sun.

"Oh, Aunt Barb. She's fine, I guess." Then Barbie looked at Gene meaningfully: "But I haven't seen her in several years. She...Aunt Barb's been married four times, you know."

"No, I didn't know that. Well, you sure look like her. It's amazing. Just as pretty. Prettier."

"Thank you."

"I mean it–you're...." Gene couldn't come up with a word which would come close to expressing what he felt. "I suppose I'd better mingle. Lots of catching up to do. So long, Barbie," Gene said, at last excusing himself, and thinking about his own two marriages. "Happy Trails," he added, but she didn't seem to get the reference.

For a moment, Gene yet lingered in Barbie's company. Bruce was no longer looking, and Gene thought of asking Barbie even more about, not Barb, but her own life. He wanted to know more about her–but having already said goodbye twice, no doubt starting up once more would strike the girl as odd, or aggressive. Gene, you know, was essentially kind, just not always appropriate. He was essentially shy. And now Bruce was looking again.

Besides, Gene also had more to say to Susie, that girl he'd barely known prior to the previous night, and still barely knew despite everything.

She wasn't immediately locatable, among the three hundred or so gathered reunioners, spouses, and children. The crowd had grown, and it was noisy, like a political rally.

"Have you seen Susie Barstow?" he said to Epstein.

"Who?"

"Susie Barstow. You Byrd?"

"Is that her?" Byrd pointed to a woman in the middle of a circle of friends, laughing and carrying on.

That was her. Lively, bright, tallish, sweet. She was chatting. How much Gene wished his own son had been able to attend so as he could introduce him to her. Gene felt she would like him. Gene liked her, that was for sure.

He disengaged her for a second.

"Are you okay?" she said.

"I'm good."

She laughed. "A minute ago you looked like you were going to explode."

The Love Interest

"PEOPLE DON'T MAKE lasting friendships after they turn twenty-five."

Thus argued Tully Gilchrist–not the famous Tully Gilchrist–as Jill, on his boat that summer evening in Sausalito, looked out at the sea. They'd already made love.

They had become acquainted but earlier in the day at Red Rock Beach, Tully arriving a short time after Jill and her friend, Janey, and proceeding to set his towel down right beside them, then stripping off his clothes slowly, nonchalantly–shirt, shoes, socks, the rest. He stood for a long moment looking around. Jill watched what she considered to be a kind of performance. He stretched. Slicked back his graying hair. Applied sun screen to his front side. Every action seemed done in an exaggerated fashion. None of it accidental, she suspected.

It was late June and beyond the fog line a few warmish days were at last available. That morning, heading north on Route 101, across Golden Gate, past Sausalito, turning onto 1–the famous Route 1–the girls had come to the fork in the road, right toward Muir Woods and left toward the ocean. Jill veered left. She enjoyed winding up and down through the valley, past the Zen Center and Muir Beach and Slide Ranch, and then way above the sea like riding a tidal wave. Yellow wildflowers bloomed just beyond the edge of the highway. The girls listening to their favorite rock station, Janey singing along–actually shouting the lyrics, reaching across Jill at musical intervals to tap the car horn. "You're the designated driver," Janey said, opening a beer, still singing.

But as they neared their destination the station grew a bit staticky and weak. And the cell phone by Jill's side was in a "no service available" mode.

It was Janey's idea to go to Red Rock. "A right of passage," she said, raising her eyebrows. "Will do a bit of trolling. Bound to be plenty of boys there, Jilly. Men even. Straight ones–with one thing on their mind."

"One thing, if that," said Jill.

The girls broke into laughter. They had known each other only a few weeks, but they had become fast, friends, sisterly. Seeming, as girls often did, a little bit lesbian.

They stayed in jeans and long-sleeved tops for the hike down to the beach– the Bay Guardian's guide to nude beaches had warned of poison oak. The hike itself was lovely, curving along the cliff, the sea blue in the distance or blue-green, the waves hatching, the sun bright on the flowers and red-tinged leaves of the weeds. Tame-seeming lizards crossed on the path before the girls into sweet-smelling brush. Halfway down they stopped to take in the horizon and catch their breath–distant cruise ships, like painted cutouts, riding on the edge. Jill felt both free and anxious as she looked on: the morning indissoluble, gaping open; the pelicans banking, divebombing; the ships seemingly sailing into nowhere. "Ode to the ends of the earth," she said to herself, not knowing exactly what she meant by the thought, but in California she often had feelings of freedom and anxiousness simultaneously–as though life promised more than it did in other places, and as though California were taking the measure of her, a girl from the Midwest. The idea of sailing to the ends or even off the edge of the earth had a certain appeal, a certain romantic, almost apocalyptic force.

They arrived at the beach, and there before them, turned over like stones, were bodies, white bodies mostly–some reclining, some wading in the surf, and a few poised statue-like on the huge grayish-blue and rust colored rocks. It became apparent that this last group was made up of young Hispanic men, still clothed, who had come to gawk, drink, and hang with their buddies. A twelve pack of Budweiser, torn open, was community property. A couple of the young men were shirtless–light flashing off their collar bones. Nonetheless Jill couldn't help but wish at least one of them would take all his clothes off. Their separate-ness was both a challenge and an affront. They were playing by different rules, living by a different code, working from a different model. Getting naked in front of their buddies a violation.

Still, she was in no hurry herself to get naked. A few women were there, most with partners, and a couple of young families, but men dominated the scene. Janey, unconcerned, had her clothes off like that, crossing her arms in front of her chest and quickly yanking off her tank top, then slipping down her pants, her underpants. She was an attractive young woman, blond, already tan, and trimmed, a small, narrow, feathery patch of blond pubic hair float- ing plankton- like on her smooth skin. She opened two beers, handing one to Jill, who drank thirstily, though what Jill really craved was a chai latte, a drink she'd been doing since coming to San Francisco. She was glad to be out of the city—there was something on the beach which went beyond mere voyeurism, or exhibitionism, some sort of desire to be surrounded by unadorned, funda- mental nature—but the city offered a regulated form of exchange, of needs and pleasures, she also required. Yet when she at last, resigned, took off her shirt, bra, jeans, and panties (sitting down on blanket to do so), she felt suddenly free and not so anxious. Strangely unanxious. "Ode to this," she thought. "Ode to the coves, and the white scales of the sea near the breakers. Ode to Route 1, the gently modulated landscape, green and queer and...kelp brown. Ode to tides, and to...well, that attractive man next to me. But no ode, today, to that Mexican boy perched right above us!"

Of course he may have been looking mostly at Janey—though some do prefer short brown hair, pale skin, and a tomboyish figure, like Jill's.

Janey didn't seem to mind the boy gargoyle on the cliff above them. "He's just getting his groove on," she said.

But another man, older, not Hispanic, and apparently alone, was filming. The girls, close to the rocks, were a prime object of his attention. They were oblivi- ous to his presence, as apparently the others on the beach were as well. Janey was occupied with two guys who'd come over to welcome them to Red Rock. These regulars ("losers?" thought Jill) were in their late thirties or early forties. However both were fit—shortly before they'd been playing beach frisbee—and, to Jill's surprise, both were shaved near hairless, hairless as Asians, which served to emphasize their darkly tanned, slug-like penises. One of them was talking about the "Grand Fixed Cross," meaning that certain planets were in opposition and so big things were in store, not necessarily good, for all fixed signs, Aquarius, Leo, etc. Jill meanwhile tried to read the book she'd brought along, a biography of Frida Kahlo, her hero.

"Frida and Diego lived for a time in San Francisco," Tully said, and she looked up. Jill tilted her head and shaded her eyes but even then, in the bright sunlight, she couldn't see him perfectly. His was a squarish face, but handsome. He wore a short, trimmed beard; it was flecked with gray. He was nearly twice her age, Jill guessed. "A quite beautiful mural of Rivera's is in The City Club, have you seen it?" he asked.

"Afraid I haven't," replied Jill. "I've been in the City just a few months."

"From Chicago?"

"My God, how weird. It's that obvious?"

"I have an ear for accents. I'm from the Midwest myself, Cleveland originally. Clevelanders supposedly possess the 'standard' accent, you know? But I can still hear it."

Jill laughed, and then, rising up, resting herself on her left hand, put out her right: "Jill," she said, stopping short of giving her last name.

"Jill from Chicago," he said, as if supplying it.

They shook hands. Jill could feel her breasts moving, too.

"Dr. Gilchrist," he said.

She laughed at this, involuntarily.

"Tully Gilchrist," he quickly amended. "I don't like to announce it."

"As in the famous artist?"

"I'm his son." Jill could see the resemblance, especially in the jaw–smooth, jutting, coast-like. "He died five years ago, as perhaps you recall. I'm the executor of the trust, among other things. I keep the archives orderly, the trains on time. The flame alive. And you, an artist?"

"Isn't everyone in S.F.?" Jill said, thinking about the writer's workshop she'd gone to the week before. But her comment, she felt, sounded a bit catty. "Actually I'm a word person. An editor, at a magazine. I have no originality–of my own!"

"None whatsoever?" said Tully.

A moment earlier Jill had imagined the bodies on the beach as violins and cellos left by an orchestra.

"Maybe a little," she said. "Enough to be an editor."

"I have enough to be executor," Tully said. "But I carry my sketch pad around anyway." He raised it so she could see.

Was that a picture of her shoulders? she wondered. The shoulders were slender, childlike. Later she would learn that his great desire was to paint, like his father—and indeed his father's father. Most everyone knew of the Gilchrist devotion to making art. It was the family business. Their devotion to politics, high adventure, liquor, and womanizing were also well known. They were an American family to be reckoned with, quite unlike Jill's own rather modest, if interestingly fucked up, family. Yet Jill felt some justifiable family pride: her father, whom she rarely saw—even though he lived in Sacramento—was a fine musician; and her sister was a gifted if undisciplined writer. Jill's own great desire was to write. But for her sister it had come so naturally. She was a true writer—truly androgynous, a true passive/aggressive. Yet self-destructive. Jill vowed never to become like her sister, if only to protect her mother—who kept the faith in all respects—from further heartache.

"Look at those guys up on the rocks," Jill said rather abruptly, to Tully. She didn't really want to talk further about art, or writing. Or career. "There," she said.

Two young men were hanging from the sheer, volcanic cliff side, practicing their repelling. One of them was bouncing his way down.

"Hey, stop that! Put that away!" someone suddenly blurted out, but not at the climbers. A heavy-set woman stood naked above the lounging crowd, shouting, staring up at the rocks. Her son, about fourteen, and her daughter, about twelve, also naked, were standing beside her. Perhaps it was the repellers who'd brought attention to the man with the camera. At any rate, now he was the object of many eyes, and a fair amount of scorn, standing there in his crevice, himself naked—and bald, Jill noticed—the video camera hanging down at his side. And soon several men were making their way toward him. "Excuse me for a minute," Tully said to her and, without being recruited, joined the others. He sprung up from his spot on the beach in a flash, quickly climbing the uneven rocks, the men appearing happy to have something to exercise themselves on. Tully was the tallest of them—and, Jill felt, the most impressive figure, the most imposing. He had a strong, muscular back. She imagined herself running her hand across the furrow of his spine. She even allowed herself to imagine, for a moment, that Tully was her man, her protector—her knight in "shiny" armor, she joked to herself, thinking about his skin, the lovely worn sea shell appearance she'd noticed when he was up close.

But now he was some thirty feet away and she couldn't hear most of what was said. Dr. Gilchrist appearing to be actively involved in the negotiations.

The incident led to Tully gaining possession of the video tape, although he said nothing about it until later, when, at his suggestion, just the two of them drove to his boat in Sausalito. Janey had agreed to escort Jill's Accord back to their flat in the city. "You can drive all right?" Jill asked. "I'll be fine. I've only had two," said Janey (she didn't mention that first she was going over to a regular's house, nearby, for a hot tub, although Jill had an guessed as much).

"That guy refused to erase the film so I tore it from the camera," Tully said, as they drove, slowly, taking the coast route as she had done some three hours earlier. Jill looked out over the flat, rounded watery horizon, the surface like the shiny plastic of an old record album. For a moment, she was back in Chicago, looking out on Lake Michigan. For a moment, her father was by her side, but only for a moment.

Her father? Who was he really.

As for Tully's actions, she wasn't sure she approved. Further, she was wondering how he'd been able to hide the tape when he had no clothes on. And how he'd been able to convince the other men to leave it in his possession—though he was the last to return. She determined that she would press him about it later. Jill wanted to see Tully's boat, and see those paintings of his father's which were on the boat, and, for reasons less clear to her, see more of Tully. After the beach incident she'd taken a short walk, to pee, and there among the huge rocks, the surf rushing up the cove and then receding, she'd felt in the presence of something fundamental and primordial, even believing, for a moment, that she felt a small earthquake tremor, or aftershock, or the swift, smooth movement of a passing shark—and for some reason she attached these feelings to Tully Gilchrist. Or was it the Tully Gilchrists?

The harbor was lovely, and quiet. They walked past a long series of boats, most of them painted white, although many of the sails were down and covered with bright blue tarps. Tully's boat was not by any stretch of the imagination the nicest boat. Or even a very nice boat, outside. It was a fifties boat, a complete lapse in good taste. The wood was half rotted. "My slip," Tully said, when they'd come to the far end of the wooden pier. Jill looked at the name on the back of the boat. "The Love Interest," it read, the curling red letters against a white background faded to a lipstick kiss.

"'The Love Interest,' eh?" she said.

"You know the painting?"

"Your father's? Now that you mention it, I think maybe I do. A young boy on a shoreline?"

"Yes. Eyeing a rowboat. I was the boy. The model for it. I never understood the title completely though! Do you?"

"Not if you don't!" Jill said.

"The old man never explained and I was too scared to ask. Maybe just a kind of joke—loving a boat more than a woman. Made it easy to name my boat, anyway."

Tully unlocked the portal door and stepped inside, but just as she was about to step forward after him the wind rose and the boat pulled away from the pier. Tully caught her in his arms. He kissed her. First her neck, then her lips. Then her neck again. She felt herself swooning, like a school girl. Like a groupie. She kissed him back. He kissed the top of her breasts.

"So you're not working from the friendship model, I see," Jill said.

"Not exactly. I prefer the seduction model. A family tradition, I guess. The like-father- like-son model."

Once aboard, she saw, above his desk, the picture they had just spoken of.

"This is a smaller study," he said. "The bigger version is at the Chicago Art Institute."

Yes, that was where she had seen it, and it struck her how odd that now she was with the son of the painter. Almost as though she were with the painter himself.

"The bigger version doesn't clear up the title ambiguity, of course," Tully said, smiling a boyish smile. "In fact, it exaggerates it!"

Jill could see he enjoyed, in his own fashion, being the son of a great painter.

The interior of the boat was beautifully done, the appointments clean, the furnishings a nice complement of formica, wood, and brass. The carpet was white, as was the davenport. A bamboo chair with ottoman was obviously Tully's reading chair. Since it was a large boat, a fifty footer, the interior was a livable-size space, yet intimate. Sun flooded the windows. Jill thought of the Frank Lloyd Wright houses and churches she'd visited in and around Oak Park, the buildings, she felt, almost as much a part of their environment as a boat at sea.

"Wine? A cup of chai?" Tully said.

Jill, startled, look at him: "Oh, chai, please. With honey, if you have it?"

"I do," he said.

So when they made love, an hour later, Jill was sober, only one beer under her belt and that from much earlier. Visions of naked bodies, and of the sea and sand, were before her eyes as Tully, a large man, peeled off her pale blue top and then her jeans and took her right there on the couch, deep in the cushions. Having already seen her naked was it as exciting for him, she wondered? It seemed to be exciting enough.

She'd been around middle-aged men. She'd seen the way they acted around young women. It was sort of pathetic, yet it excited her. Even the gay man who ran the writer's workshop, Michael Richie, famous in his own right, had singled her out for special attention. Jill was the only woman in the group that night—another woman was gone on vacation—and the men, most of them straight, were nothing to "write home about," Jill had thought to herself, too clever by half. "Oh, darling," Michael had said, interrupting himself to address her, as he would do throughout the evening, interrupting a long monologue of criticism, reminiscence, backbiting, and adulation of the truly great—Proust, Emily Bronte, Nabokov—to say, at that one point, "Oh, darling, don't chew on your pencil, you'll mar those lovely lips." Jill had only stayed for a single session.

Tully had finished pretty fast; but not too fast. He was expert, she thought, yet carried away all the same. Just as he was coming, pounding her, he whispered, breathlessly in her ear, "Oh, Jill. Jill, I want your twenties, girl." That was all she needed–she was there, his. At least for the moment. They rolled over, time having nicely slowed down, for both of them.

Jill, thinking of his words a bit later, took it as a thought forged in the heat of the moment. Yet what was she going to do with her twenties? At present she wasn't all that excited by the prospects, not even all that excited about living in San Francisco–an attitude that Janey found strange, if not pitiful. "You've got to take more interest in your own generation. You're an Xer," said Janey. Jill agreed with her–she'd loved *Pulp Fiction* for example–but on the whole she felt vaguely lost in time, or nostalgic for something she couldn't quite name. Maybe it was the material universe itself, its texture, its thisness, unmistakableness, she missed. And who could say, maybe Tully could find better uses for her twenties than she could? Though to put it in those terms caused Jill to feel slightly ashamed.

After sex, they drank. And Tully stepped out on the deck for a smoke. Jill didn't smoke–his cigarette looked like a tiny rocket burning in his hand. It was a beautiful if slightly blustery evening. She noticed that up close the water was green, but far off it was gray, shark- gray. Of all the boats in the harbor, his was nearest the open sea.

"Why did you want the video, Tully?" she said. "Afraid of a famous son caught in a compromising position?

"I hadn't thought of that. You can't be too careful, I suppose. Maybe he was the paparazzi!"

"Well, then why?" she persisted.

It was then that Tully, unresponsively, said what he did about lasting friendships being rare after someone turns twenty-five. Jill wasn't even twenty-five so she didn't have any basis for evaluating his statement. If it was true, then her friendship with Janey had a chance of lasting–though of course the inverse of his statement wasn't in play, that is, friendships made before twenty-five necessarily last. And what if one person is under twenty-five and one over?

"Perhaps the older you get the more you need those who have known you for a long time, or during formative stages," Tully continued. "Or maybe it's because when you're young you don't so much choose your friends as hang out with those with whom you share your life, in the neighborhood, or on the baseball team, or just inside the school on a wintry day. I suspect is isn't all that different for marriage. If you marry the farm girl down the road or the girl from your parish, as soon as high school is finished, and you struggle together, you might just have a chance. A lack of choice is the essential thing. Maybe the only thing. If you choose your spouse, you're doomed."

Jill wanted to ask: "Have you been married?" And: "More than once?" Hadn't his father married three times? And she wanted to ask, too: "What's your sign?" She herself was an Aquarian. Further, she wanted to quibble with his pronouncement—for wasn't love itself beyond choice to begin with?

Around eight o'clock the sun began to sink. Jill watched it spangled white on the water just as she had watched sunsets on similar summer nights along Lake Michigan. Her mother, back home, living alone now, would be expecting to hear from her tomorrow morning, Sunday morning. Jill always called. Her mother, who came to Chicago from Lithuania, had never really adapted to the new world—and of course she wouldn't stand for certain things. Jill would call. Yet there was really no question but that she would spend the night with Tully.

When the wind picked up some more, they went inside. The fog, regathering, was banked along the thick tree-lined hillside. Inside they were warm, cozy, safe. Tully put on a jazz record, Bill Evans.

But one question hadn't really been answered. "So?" Jill said. Tully—Dr. Gilchrist—looked at her. "The video?" she said.

"I was afraid I'd never see you again," he said.

"Later you can tell me a true story," Jill said, smiling.

The cabin bedroom was just large enough for a standard double bed. Jill looked at herself in the mirror above the bed. She was slightly sunburned. Her neck and cleavage were brighter than the rest, except for her butt, which was almost the color of pink grapefruit. She snuggled up under Tully's arm.

Again she thought of Michael Richie. How rude he was that brilliant writer. How prideful. How vain—though certainly entertaining.

"Ladies and gentlemen," he would always begin, though occasionally modified, for Jill's sake, to "Lady and Gentlemen," so beginning, "Lady and Gentlemen," always, Jill felt, sort of beginning over, or again. Beginning the beginning, sort of. Something had led him to the movie, *Sunset Boulevard*, at one particular moment. "Remember that line from *Sunset Boulevard* when Gloria

Swanson has taken William Holden out to buy some new clothes and he is about to choose a mohair coat and the tailor says, 'Well, if the lady is buying, if the lady is buying you might as well get the vicuna.' The vicuna, ladies and gentlemen! And just then William Holden sees himself in the mirror, mind you. The hustler caught in his own reflection. I once saw Billy Wilder in a restaurant, on Polk Street, and well I'd just won the same award as he had—the Pen Award—and I thought of going up to him and saying, 'Oh, Mr. Wilder, we just won the same award.'" "Did you do it?" one participant said. "Oh, no. I would never be so rude. Sometimes people will come up to me and say, 'Are you still hustling?' Can you believe such rudeness, ladies and gentlemen."

Yet no one got in a word edgewise during the workshop. If someone's comment went on too long Richie would tap the edge of his water glass. That meant it was time for Michael Richie to speak again.

"Do you think you have to be an asshole, be crazy, to be a great artist?" Jill asked Tully. Surely, he would know.

Tully sat up in bed. He lit a cigarette.

"Yes," he said at last.

It was not the answer Jill was expecting and not what she wanted to hear.

"Self-expression is insanity. But perhaps this is not the time for this discussion."

"Well, I don't think you have to be crazy."

"You don't, eh?"

"Yes."

"Good for you."

"Are you being sarcastic?" Jill said.

"No. I guess you just need to be brave. Be willing to stand alone." Tully suddenly held her, tight.

But only for a little while. Once his cigarette was finished, he turned over on his side.

"I dream better when I don't touch. I don't touch at the movies either. Don't want to break the spell," he said.

He looked tired, his age, Jill thought. She was a bit whipped herself. The fresh air and the hike, the wine and the sex, and an odd sense of finishing off certain things left Jill drained, relaxed—yet somehow also alert, exhilarated, like she'd played a long game of scrabble and suddenly had scrabbled out, getting rid of an "x" or "z." She half wanted to fall asleep and half wanted to party. "Zombie," she thought to herself.

Rising from Tully's bed, she went into the nearly dark living area. Perhaps, really, she should leave. It would be easy enough to walk to downtown Sausalito and from there catch a cab for the short ride over the bridge to San Francisco, a San Francisco which suddenly seemed to beckon to her. In fact, she saw herself returning not just to San Francisco but to Chicago, saw herself spiriting across the country into the heartland, like one of Jack Kerouac's maniacs. Yet it was close to midnight, and it was cool out—windy, the boat rocking gently, moving slowly back and forth like a pendulum. The ropes were creaking. Morning would come soon enough, no? She could leave then, if she still wanted to.

She turned on Tully's desk lamp. There, on his desk, rested the video. Without hesitating she popped it in the VCR, at the same time pressing down the volume button. But just as she was about to sit down, on the floor, another idea occurred to her—a writer's idea, which she suspected had been there all along. Jill set the vcr on pause, pausing it so happened, though not surprisingly, on the first shots of her body and Janey's body. To see herself naked on film that way was a bit of a shock. The white beach provided a grainy, canvas-like background. The cameraman had zoomed in. Tully was also in the frame, but, oddly, he appeared to be staring up at the camera. Jill felt she would need to investigate this more thoroughly, later, but right then she was a hurry. She opened the portal door and quickly slipped outside. The wind was strong. The masts were chiming and shaking, their reflections casting white arrows down into the black water. In the dark, the sea seemed to smell sharper. Next to the pier a jelly fish was visible, its lovely, translucent form fanning open and then closed and then open again, leaving Jill, for a moment, almost mesmerized.

But then hurriedly if calmly—enjoying her fight with the wind—she loosened the six mooring ropes. Tully's boat sprung quickly, surely free, like a wild horse unbridled, unharnessed. Jill gave out a sharp whoop which echoed across the water. Already the boat was moving. Quickly once more, she leapt back on board—just catching the railing of the back deck and lifting herself to safety. When she saw lights from two other boats flick on, she was a bit unnerved. But blessedly, Tully was apparently still asleep.

The tv screen was blank. The VCR had turned itself off. Jill pressed the play button once again and curled up on the davenport. She glanced out the windows of the boat: it appeared that the boat next to theirs was moving but Jill knew otherwise—she could feel movement beneath her. The grand, fixed movement of the world, she was thinking. Soon they'd be at sea. She imagined the boat passing beneath the Golden Gate as though beneath the shadow of a god.

Almost all of the video tape was, as it turned out, of her body not Janey's. Tully was seen smiling, sometimes looking up at the camera and sometimes elsewhere. Even on the video he looked imposing, impressive. Jill watched until the end. She was saying goodbye. There was really no choice.

Evolution

THE INTIMACY I shared with the girls in the booth in front of me was disturbed. They had been talking about their boyfriends for the longest time, for ages. It was not very intelligent conversation they offered, but it was interesting–it took me back. Their sense of self and their lives were of a piece, nothing double had broken in. Life and their view of life ran parallel, were virtually the same. They were barely old enough to be in the bar, Fast Ethel's, in San Diego, barely old enough, if that. They even chalked up their mistakes to "experience." I listened to them, pretending to read my book, and sipping a glass of burgundy. I listened like an aural voyeur; their talk was enough to fill in the pictures. The blond coiffured one had recently given in to her boyfriend. "I had to sometime," she said. But then, as I said, the picture-making was disturbed. A woman (whom I'd seen come in in my basketball peripheral vision) was weaving toward me where I sat at the back of the bar. I could only see her outline because the light from the window shone from behind her, like in a religious painting. As she came closer her face suddenly appeared below the imitation kerosene lamp which hung a few feet in front of me. She looked like a white monkey. Initially I distrusted this image I'd conjured up; I'd been spending my afternoons at the San Diego Zoo. But as she came closer it was clear: her close-shaved head and her large ears and thick lips had monkey written all over them. She looked to be about forty; perhaps she was younger and well used. She presented an incalculable contrast to the girls in front of me, who were forced to resist her attempts to sit down with them. She sat with me instead. Her frown broke into a big-toothed grin.

"Beautiful day," she said.

"Yes," I mumbled. It was a beautiful end of March day, but I didn't know if, considering her drunken condition, she was just kidding.

"Do you mind if I sit with you?" she said.

"No, it's all right."

"Can I get you another beer?" she offered next, not noticing my, still half-full, glass of wine.

"No thanks," I said, politely.

"It's your uptight Long Island Jewishness, is't it?"

I must say I was taken aback.

"Well, I'm not Jewish, though my mother's from Queens, if that counts. But she's Catholic. I was raised Methodist myself."

"You're not Jewish? You look like a handsome young Jewish boy."

There was little I could say to that. I'd never been taken for a Jew. "Are you Jewish?" I asked, but she immediately started to laugh.

"No, not me, I only wish I was."

Once more I didn't know quite what to say. The blond in the next booth gave me a consolatory look.

"At times I've wanted to be Catholic," I said at last, acknowledging the desire to be what we're not. "Especially now around Easter time."

"You can have my membership in the Universal Church," she said, again breaking into her big-toothed smile.

"Too much to believe in," I said, and she nodded in agreement.

"Are you from New York then?" she asked.

"No. Indiana and Arizona."

"Indiana? Where?"

"West Lafayette. Boilermaker country."

"Do you know the Fitzgerald Construction Company?"

"Sure, Mike McNeill was a friend of mine. His mom owned the business, right?"

"Right. Old J.J. McNeill never owned it, even though he acts like it. I was the bohemian who married Richard Fitzgerald, Mike's uncle and Betty's brother."

"Betty, Mike's mom."

"Yes. She was actually quite decent to me."

"How amazing. Small world, isn't it? You're not married to him now?"

"No," she said, her eyes wet and red from drinking, "that was ten years ago. I live in San Diego with my daughter and old man. She just turned twelve."

"From your first marriage, to Fitzgerald?"

"Yes. That bastard."

"My daughter is four," I said, and waited for the usual reaction. She didn't believe it. "A high school marriage," I said. "When we separated, Sarah, my Ex, tried to kill herself," I added, immediately regretting the intimacy.

"My daughter is a beautiful child," she continued, looking at me, considering what I had said, "beautiful, but stubborn. She's crazy about boys but won't give an inch, no compromises. None. It's not easy."

I assumed the last remark referred to the job of raising her daughter. I could picture her daughter. I pictured her blond and pretty unlike monkey woman. I guess the blond girl in the next booth was affecting my imagination.

"Where is your daughter?" she asked.

"With her mother in Phoenix. I hope to have her for a month this summer."

"In San Diego?"

"Well, if I'm still here. I've been here over a year already. I've traveled this wonderful parallelogram from Phoenix to Tucson to L.A. to San Diego. I don't know what it means but I like the symmetry. I may go back to teaching in Tucson, to grad school. I'm crazy for knowledge."

"If you have her for a month," she said, returning to the original subject, wanting to make a point (and I think unimpressed by my flippancy), "in a month the newness wears off."

"Yes, we all suffer, don't we," I said and laughed in hopes of heading off a long sorrowful discussion of her homelife. She was enough to handle right then. I didn't want to deal with a maudlin drunk, although I was aware of certain advantages—she might be just the one to cure me of the priestly celibacy I'd indulged in over the previous few months. I had never been with an older woman and I felt it might do both of us some good. At least she might be able to treat it as a one-night stand, an ability probably foreign to the blond girl and her companion (who continued to chat and order more beer). Of course I wasn't sure I wanted monkey woman, assuming she wanted me. It was not just her drunkenness, it was the deteriorated condition of her body as well, that gave me second thoughts. She had clearly put herself through a lot.

"I need another beer," she said. "Don't leave," she pleaded.

"I won't...but maybe you don't need another one."

"Now you're just being silly," she said and wandered over to the bar. She took a stool to wait for her beer. Meanwhile the blond girl's friend suddenly got up and left "to go to class." I expected the blond to follow because I couldn't imagine her sitting alone in a bar. But she stayed to finish her beer and read a magazine.

Monkey woman returned, barely returned before collapsing.

"Well...," she began, but paused.

"Jack," I said, "and yours?"

"Peggy. So Jack, what are you doing in San Diego?"

"I work in the mornings. I'm a gardener at a restaurant. I write in the afternoon or got to the zoo. At night I dream about weeds."

"You're a writer," Peggy said emphatically. "Isn't that something. I'm a reader, a reading junkie." Then, however, there was a pause. I'm also a gardener and zoo-goer, I almost said. "Read any good books lately?" she said, joking.

"No, not lately. I just started *Sons and Lovers* and I like that."

"Do you read Commentary? You should," she went on not waiting for my answer (which would have been the negative). "They are the best. You're young and you should be educated. I've had this fantasy about the editorial departments of big magazines, New York Review of Books, New Republic, Commentary. At the New York Review they cut each other up. One week it's one group of editors, then another. At New Republic they all sit down together, all very pleasant. At Commentary they do both, you get it all." Peggy pulled a nose-dropper from her purse and shot it up her nose. I didn't know if it was decongestant or what. She continued. "I mean there seems to be certain issues. Should we run in and take the oil—that's one. Myself, I want to go to Israel. It's so clear-cut there. So clear-cut."

"What do you mean?" I said, at the same time acknowledging a smile from the blond girl, a smile of "Yes, we've all been trapped, what can you do?" Just like with your boyfriend, I thought, and looked at her. She glanced back down at her magazine.

"I mean this," Peggy said. "I mean I try to be an American but it's so hard. Why do we keep putting ourselves down?" she said and looked at me with her wet eyes as if I might know the answer. "Why do we keep saying the country is going fascist? If we keep saying it, it will."

"Who's saying it?" I asked.

"It seems the best and brightest are."

"They're not always the wisest, as we know," I said, but felt uncomfortable with know-it- all sound of that statement so I added a half-hearted, "Oh, I don't know," and felt better. However my relief was short-lived. Peggy grew maudlin. She gave me a warm monkey smile.

"You are a nice boy and I'm just a sentimental old woman. Why are you sitting here letting me bring you down like this?"

"I don't know," I said again, but then politely covered myself. "I like talking to you."

I did like to talk, and I did feel for her. In a perverse way I found her interesting. I hadn't slept with a woman for quite some time, no matter what shape.

Increasingly I'd come to consider a trip to Tijuana. The fear of venereal disease kept me from going though. One night I had gone down, but I wound up spending my money on a losing jai alai player instead of a whore, some scalper's "sister." Peggy, perhaps sensing my thoughts, suddenly began to rub my hand. The blond girl looked on confused—did I actually want this woman to sit with me?

"Rubbing is a positive good," Peggy said, massaging my right hand with great felicity. "I was in Berkeley during the 60's, you know. I met Abbie Hoffman and Jerry Rubin. And I had some numbers going besides my old man. Yes, 1,2,3, some numbers. But those days are gone," she said, very sad-faced. "I've made mistakes. I mean we are just another species. You know something about evolution, right?"

"Right," I said, nearly choking on my wine. God, Peggy the monkey woman had started to talk about evolution. She went on ahead—oblivious, of course, to the way I envisioned her.

"There are no guidebooks handed out. I mean, there are some but only by the work of a prodigious mind, like Darwin's. But homoerectus, right? They could blow it all away and I don't care. I'm still proud of being a human being. Why must we always blame ourselves? But then you're so innocent and so young."

"I'm young, but not so innocent," I said directly.

Drunkenness, I believed, was not a licence for saying or doing anything. Nonetheless, my counter statement had created a kind of prayerlike silence. Peggy lit a cigarette, her cleavage brightening in the matchlight. She also needed another beer; I got up to get it for her. As I passed by, the blond girl gave me a soft almost furry smile. Perhaps giving in to her boyfriend had not proved that wonderful. But when I returned with Peggy's beer and more wine for myself, the blond had left. Like most times I had moved too slowly. I felt the old pain but also felt relieved. Peggy, in a way, had kept me from this young girl. As for Peggy, she had laid her head down on the table. She was too drunk to take home, I told myself.

"Here's your beer," I said and sat. Peggy raised her head.

"I could make you feel good," she said.

"I need to go home," I said, and grabbed my jacket. "I'd offer for you to come with me, but you're too drunk and I'm too sober and it's too far up the hill. I'd better go alone."

"You twit," she said, "it could have been possible to go home with you and you let me get this drunk."

"I'm sorry. I better go." But as I started to get up she held my hand and massaged it.

"I have an eqaulizer, you know," she said. "I have a lid."

I stood up and stood next to her, considering. I tried to picture us in bed together. I pictured her fleshy shapelessness, her close-shaven monkey head. I wasn't digusted, but neither was it appealing. Still, as she rubbed my hand, I considered it.

"Oh, fuck it," she said. "I'm not going to talk you into anything." She took her hand away. "I don't want favors."

I didn't blame her for thinking that way—homoerectus, right—but mainly I was thinking about myself. I wished she was sober. Then I was glad she wasn't. I had an excuse. I could see she needed it, but I couldn't believe she needed this, this gutteral urge. Human contact, yes, but wouldn't it be worse as soon as it was over? She massaged my thigh, and I felt my cock stiffen. She gave me a warm, sad, monkey smile. It was too much. Too close to a real monkey and at the same time too human, as a monkey is too human.

"I've got to home. I'll see you," I said.

"I doubt it," she said. "I doubt you see."

"I see you're a sentimental, horny middle-aged woman."

"You damn Catholics," she said, angrily. "Damn Catholics," she said once more, but the last time it was only a drunken mutter.

And since I hadn't been raised Catholic, there was little to say back to her.

The Strongest Man Stands Most Alone

THE TWO MEN decided to take a trip to San Francisco, to get away for a few days but also to discuss politics. Cesar had notions of starting a political party. He wasn't as a rule terribly political–and got enough of politics at the college–but one night he'd risen abruptly from his bed inspired, grabbed a yellow legal pad, and set to work, downtown LA visible to the east, the white and pastel lights from the skyscrapers shining through the fog as if an ocean liner had docked there. He had in mind a center-right/center-left coalition: anti affirmative action and pro healthcare, anti abortion and pro gun control, anti immigration and pro environment, etc. "I'm speaking for those without a voice," he felt assured.

His first, and sole, adherent however at that time was Timothy. Timothy St. James being also about his only friend in Los Angeles. He and his wife, Linda, were living up in the Hollywood Hills, a world away from the basin, in a lovely Frank Lloyd Wright-like home, which at one time had belonged to Linda's father. Cesar had his hopes that Linda would get on board as well.

Even in daylight the drive up to their place was tricky–Montgomery Cliff had crashed coming down those hills after a party–and it was dark out when Cesar left his apartment.

He'd called up on his cell phone: "Ready to roll?" When they were in the car, Cesar asked Timothy which route.

"Take 170 to the 5."

"How about wearing that seatbelt, my man."

Cesar waited, idling the car.

"Well, when in Rome," his passenger laughingly submitting at last.

After each stop Cesar forced to remind him to put it on again.

To Cesar, Timothy was Jack London, or about as close as you were likely to come, right down to the Oakland origins and the well-knit, compact build. An actor, he'd started as a dancer. He moved with a light grace. He had silver blond hair and movie star looks. And, not unlike London, was given to extreme left-right thinking, more extreme than Cesar's own. Tim—that's what Linda called him—had it in for Jews and Germans. The whole world for him was conspiratorial. A few powerful people controlled the whole shebang. His "truth"—and it was grotesque—was that big business and big government, the U.S. and Israel, Republicans and Democrats alike, not to mention the media—you name it, anyone on top—was in on it. He believed that the fall of the Berlin Wall was due to elites on each side deciding they could benefit from its destruction.

The two men talked the whole way. At first about acting not politics. About acting—who was good and who was not, and why—they pretty much agreed. Brando was god, for example. But it was about politics they needed to come to some agreement on if they were going to start a political party—not that Timothy could stay off politics for long in any case. It happened the present political conversation also involved acting. Someone had told him that actor and now governor Arnold Swartzenegger used to, in Austria, pass Nazi literature back and forth with friends. That was enough proof for Timothy, or it fit the pattern, corroborated his suspicions about Swartzenegger.

"He's a Nazi. His father was in the S.A., a brown shirt."

This latter statement was true. Indeed, Swartzenegger had paid the Simon Wiesenthal Holocaust Museum to investigate his father's war-time record. But even that was a calculated move, according to Timothy. "He gave the museum a bunch of money, of course."

Timothy was a terrifically smart guy but not scientific in his thinking. "I've been called anti-Semitic, anachronistic, uneducated," his friend to acknowledge, as they were passing through Fresno.

Timothy's only experience with college happened to be Cesar's Freshman English course, taken some four years prior, when he was already thirty-three.

On the evidence of the class, Cesar would have never hypothesized that Timothy held such strong opinions. He was respectful of both his fellow students and Cesar. Still, on one occasion, when Timothy and a girl in class, a black girl, referred to a "They" who controlled everything, he did get an inkling of his future friend's politics. "Who are 'They'?" Cesar had said, and the two of them looked at him with ironic sympathy—or worse. No doubt they considered him something of a sell-out, a coconut. Cesar did feel like a sell-out but for reasons unrelated to being Hispanic, mostly having to do with choosing teaching over writing.

He surmised that Timothy's anti-Jewish sentiments—amazingly, Linda was half- Jewish—were most likely due to bad experiences in New York and Hollywood than to the actions of Israel. Timothy was a talented actor but only intermittently employed, only minimally successful. He was a kind of Palestinian in "Jewish Hollywood," at the mercy of lame and evil popular culture productions which, he believed, the Jews were largely responsible for foisting on the public. But Timothy's imagination also frequented in sentimental tropes. He was an old- school nationalist, or populist.

He argued for the little guy. He was totally pro-Muslim, pro-Palestinian. He took a certain pride in having been told by Arabs, when he traveled in the Middle East, that he was like them.

One time, in Egypt, he'd been asked what he thought of President Mubarak.

"'I haven't met the man,' I told them. 'Ah, you're Muslim,' they said. 'No, Christian,' I said. But they insisted that I thought like a Muslim. It's a one-on-one religion, open, man to man. They're sweet-natured people. Gracious people. Women are safe on the streets. And it's a universal religion, like Buddhism and Catholicism. Not exclusive, like Judaism. People like to call Israel a democracy—the only democracy in the Middle East—but obviously it's a religious state. You have to be Jewish."

Cesar got the feeling that in the Middle East, among Palestinians, Timothy had felt at home. Arab men had told him that they were charged with a deep responsibility toward their multiple wives.

"Yeah, the Arabs just like the Mormons, created a system for taking multiple brides. Which I favor, by the way! But I've no illusions," Cesar countered.

"That's not what they told me," his friend responded. "I looked in their eyes. I saw they meant what they said."

"The Egyptians would kill for real democracy. Real opportunity," Cesar continued.

"You haven't been there," Timothy responded, Cesar thinking about how his Japanese girlfriend some years back would say "You have to go there" when he'd talk to her about Japan based on Japanese novelists he liked (Kawabata preeminently).Timothy was often flying off to places to see for himself the facts on the ground. Linda apparently didn't object to, indeed largely funded, such adventures. He'd recently returned from Bosnia.

But as far as Cesar could see, Timothy was willing to believe virtually any sort of first- hand testimonial–provided it fit his truth, fit the pattern, fit in with his overall conspiracy theory.

His father, a career Army man, had died in Vietnam when Tim was ten. He revered his father. "I'm with you," Timothy had said to Cesar when first presented with the political platform–and then had started talking about the traditional values his father had instilled in him, such as "Don't cry till it hurts."

"What does Linda think of the platform?" Cesar ventured now, as they drove.

Cesar liked Linda. Her father, now deceased, had been a Hollywood sound man. Her mother was Italian. Linda had been raised Catholic.

"She said she's for it, too," Timothy answered. "But I said to her: 'What about abortion? You don't favor limiting that?'"

"That was just instinctive, on my part," Cesar quickly inserted. "Not wholly rational, or reasoned out. Maybe it's my suppressed, mystical Catholicism coming back to haunt me."

Timothy had also been raised Catholic. He lived by codes. That a man's word was his bond, was his chief code.

The two men arrived in the Bay Area late afternoon. The boat, which belonged to Cesar's brother, was in a beautiful marina in Sausalito. But the boat itself was not beautiful really and not nearly as expensive as some of the others, which were yachts. Still, it was nice to be on the water. Cesar had grown up in desert

Phoenix and was something of a landlubber. Since moving to LA, however, he'd come more and more to feel at home near the ocean. In time, he thought he might become an old sea dog himself–reclaim his mother's Portugese roots.

The next day brought an Oakland A's game, which they attended with Timothy's son, Michael; Michael's girlfriend, Christina; and Timothy's grandson, Forest. Forest, eleven, was spending the summer with his dad. During the school year Forest lived in Iowa with his mom and stepdad, attending Maharishi International Private School and University. That summer Forest was getting a chance to play baseball.

Michael, a former high school pitcher, coached the team.

"Forest is a little bit behind," Michael confided. It was a warm day. They sat along the first base line, concrete "Mt. Davis" blocking out any possibility of a breeze. Forest was sitting a couple of rows down with his girl cousin, Chandler (ten to his eleven). "But he's catching up quickly," Michael added.

At the Maharishi school Forest played soccer. And twice a day they meditated. They even had their own form of math. The school had identified Forest as overactive, or as being what they called a Pitta type, which was creative but unbalanced, causing anger, hostility. Pitta took over people, even other types, between two a.m. and six a.m. in the morning when most people are asleep and dreaming. Pitta fills our dreams. Forest had Pitta in the daytime. He needed more Kapha.

Yet he seemed, to Cesar, a sweet little boy. Even mild, sort of feminine–as a result perhaps of the school's training. Still he was also all boy, never stopping for a minute, always on the go. At the ballpark he was often up out of his seat or teasing Chandler. Chandler, a beautiful child, blond, slender as an aspen, gave him back what he gave, tit for tat–though Cesar noticed at one point that she was pouting, her chin resting on her arms folded on the back of an empty bleacher seat.

After the game–the A's lost–everyone retreated to Michael's house for a barbecue. Barbecues were nothing new to Cesar. His own extended family never needed an excuse for a party–Hispanics wanting one thing above all, familiarity.

Michael was in charge of the hamburgers and wieners. "Just relax, Dad," he said. So Cesar and Timothy tossed a baseball back and forth. Both men had strong arms, though Cesar had never developed a curve, or really any pitch other than a fastball. Timothy had a curve and a slider; he seemed to know how to do just about everything expertly. He knew fishing and ranching and carpentry. He'd worked as a house painter and a car salesman. Cesar didn't know so much. He knew literature, and baseball some. He knew art, but Timothy also knew art–and of course theater. Once upon a time in North Beach he'd directed a long-running play about the "Beats." Not to mention the guy rode a motorcycle. He had fathered two children, both out of wedlock (Michael one of them, of course). He liked to drink and had in the past pushed drugs. Cesar, for his part, had chosen limited success and safety. He had been either a student or a teacher his entire life. Not even a writer, though he still had ideas he might yet become one someday. For a short time in his twenties he'd written fiction. He referred to that time as his "creative writing years." All he lacked back then–right, Cesar?– was a Neil Cassidy, a muse. He should have met Timothy back then, when they were young, and fresh. Cesar had written a dissertation, on D.H. Lawrence. But he'd never got around to revising it for possible publication. He wasn't a writer, he was a reader.

Maybe he'd do something in politics. But he doubted it. His politics was sex.

During the barbecue he kept one eye on Christina, Michael's girlfriend. She was Mexican- American, from Texas, and Cesar had intentionally never had much to do with "Hispanic" girls. Most of them had too much attitude–hauteur.

Timothy said of Christina: "Michael sure likes them mean."

"Perhaps she's looking for someone to put her in her place," Cesar joked.

Christina was attractive though, and young–she had the most beautiful dark eyes–and she was well read, a big plus. She mentioned Salmon Rushdie, but said she was struggling with the novel of his she was reading. She didn't like how in the novel one person became another person and then another, etc., until you didn't know about whom you were reading. Cesar also watched Chandler and Forest run back and forth.

Some neighbors showed up. They were all rabid A's fans. All had been to the game. Some had on the team colors, green and yellow. It was A's country. But after dissecting the game, and the A's chances of winning the wild-card and making the playoffs, the conversation turned to drug experiences–stories and reminiscence. Cesar had little to contribute. He'd tried marijuana a few times, of course, but he didn't like it. He didn't like how it seemed to disperse his ego. Weed made him feel like he'd become part of the woodwork, like he was no longer really there. He liked alcohol, it brought out his personality–there was more Cesar. But it, his lack of attraction to drugs, was strange nonetheless. There was something conservative in it.

So when Christina, playing hostess, retreated to the kitchen, Cesar followed. She stood at the sink rinsing fruit, her short black hair in the evening light shiny as cat fur.

"You're pretty quiet," she said. "Are you having a good time?"

"I am now," Cesar said.

"You've got a good throwing arm."

"Thanks."

"I like that in a man," she joked.

"As an A's fan."

"You don't do drugs though, huh."

"I didn't get the drug gene, I guess." Nor the magic gene either, he thought to himself. He didn't care for magical realism, despite the natural tendencies of his people. He didn't believe in religion. He didn't even like to watch magic tricks. He thought kids who practiced magic tricks were creepy.

"And you're opposed to Affirmative Action, too?"

"Word spreads," Cesar responded.

"It's all in the family."

Forest came out of the bathroom just then.

"My turn, Forest," Cesar said. And then to Christina: "I got the alcohol gene."

"Of course. You're Mexican, right?"

He didn't correct her. And of course he was, half.

Later, back at the boat, it was time–or time again–for politics.

At the ball game Timothy had repeated the Swartzenegger story to the guy on Cesar's right. So Cesar had had to sit there between two opinionated Scots-Irish guys while the word "Nazi" was kicked around like a Hacky Sack bag or something. Cesar didn't care much for Swartzenegger, but he didn't believe in name calling, in defaming someone, especially when the epithet was "Nazi." The Christian Right needed a boogie man, a devil to accuse, as reassurance of their own existence. He continued to suspect Timothy of having the same mind set–though the enemy was anyone in power in his case.

The two men sat on the deck on the back of the boat. Even though it was eight p.m., there was still some daylight. But the fog, like a giant, was emerging over the steep hillside to the west.

Timothy was scheduled to fly back to L.A. the next morning. Christina and Forest would be by the boat to pick him up (Michael had to be at work). Timothy wanted to get back to lead some final negotiations on a condo he and Linda were selling near UCLA. A fixer-upper. They were capitalists, Timothy admitting to as much. "It's just that we've lost the balance between labor and management," he'd argued, adding: "But there's no creativity in socialism." Timothy and Linda had met in North Beach some ten years prior. She was an actress who'd turned to doing real estate, which she liked–Timothy marveling that she appeared to like it better than acting. But it was tough sledding starting out. It had more ups and downs than a writer's life. More than once a "sure" sell had fallen through at the last minute. Cesar would have loved to know Linda, too, when she was young, a young, hot actress.

"I wouldn't know how to go about starting a political movement," he suddenly put in. He knew Timothy was about to broach the subject and so hoped to somehow deflect the discussion. Cesar felt embarrassed about raising the political party idea in the first place. It was out of character to make such a commitment, if on the other hand in character to use something, such as politics, to avoid writing, Timothy per-haps turning to politics as a substitute as well. "Weasel," Cesar's poet brother, Manny, had called him one time, in an email, and they hadn't spoken since, going on three years. But he felt his brother was misreading Hegel, who wrote that Shakespeare's protagonists–not Shakespeare himself!–were "free artists of themselves."

"I'm not sure people will respond?" Cesar continued, tepidly.

"Just do it," was Timothy's response. He was smoking a joint. "Run it up the flag pole and see if anyone salutes."

"But how?"

"Events. Rallies."

Timothy's desire for a public life was manifestly obvious. Through teaching, Cesar had got a taste of it, too.

"I was thinking maybe a website."

"Something safe."

Cesar laughed. "Yes. Something I don't have to be involved in."

Timothy passed him the joint. Cesar took a drag on it, maybe two, or three. He started to feel light-headed. After that he stuck to beer. Night had fallen. The water was spangled white, as if a star had shattered on its surface or were shining up from the depths.

Timothy wanted to keep talking. In fact, after he and Timothy had already discussed moral relativity and relativity in physics ("the Zionists tried to promote Einstein as the greatest genius of all time"); and gays ("people don't talk about the fact that it means one guy shoving his cock up another guy's ass"); and government lies, etc.–and each had had a couple of more beers, to Cesar's surprise Timothy started to tell the story of his life, surprising Cesar especially by the open, confessional nature of the telling. The honesty. The sharp self-analysis. The humility. The knowledge, for example, that his harsh statements were in part compensation for, among other things, the feminine nature of his profession–and he the son of a warrior. The admission, too, that he'd gone wild after his father was no longer there. And how his mother had spent, out of loyalty to his father, thirty years alone, keeping a picture of her husband above her bed. "I revered my father, but I never meant for her to do that," he said. Timothy admitted, further, that he should have probably stayed in San Francisco, running his theater. "But I got arrogant, I guess. I wanted to take on New York. To well, really be somebody."

Yes, Cesar was moved by these confessions, and impressed also by the force and manner of the presentation–indeed he was persuaded at that moment that Timothy was, when all was said and done, politics aside, among the best men he had ever met. And like Jack London, a real guy. In a tight spot Cesar felt he would be able to trust Timothy as he would trust few others. Tim was, standing there on the boat that night surrounded by the shimmering white-flecked water, someone you could believe in, a presence, bigger than life, like a great literary character, in fact. And seeing him standing there, legs splayed, astride the boat (and taller than the cabin door), Cesar felt his spirits lift, he felt exalted, the way literature sometimes made him feel exalted. Yes, his friend was an actor, a performer, a charmer–and one who, it was true, had never really found a theater of operations equal to his desire. But nonetheless he was convincing and that, Cesar felt, counted for a lot. Here was someone who had decided to stand against the tide, engaged, fearless, come what may, his emotions exposed and his heart plumb to the world.

But in the morning, hungover, awakening to the animal-like sounds of Forest padding overhead on the deck, Cesar did begin to have second thoughts. Especially when, on top of Christina's voice, he heard his friend call out to that grandson of his he hardly knew: "Come down from there this very minute, young man."

Happy Baby

AT THE LIBRARY he meant to do a little research, retired men that day already manning the computers (not a card catalog in sight), the place still a bit musty, the morning light filtering in gray as glass, the librarian at her desk—"Time like money going out the window," Frank mused aloud to us. "The men do little more than a nod to each other, keep an urinal distance."

These days Frank often found himself walking down to the public library—"waddling" actually, having never imagined the day would come when that would be the case. He was feeling a slight soreness in his hips, Dang unrelenting at the yoga class despite his nubie status. He'd come across her and Miss Denise at Starbucks a week earlier and had on his own brought up yoga (learning of it through Taylor's feed), first asking if there were any kids in the class, and then if it was all women. No, there were no kids—the class met on Friday mornings—but yes generally it was all women though Dang said her brother showed up for some sessions. Miss Denise, her Miniature Schnauzer wrapped up in her arms, described herself as a yoginubie. Dang, in her early twenties, was of mixed race (Thai and black), and lithe as a lynx. All of us were familiar with Miss Denise. Generally half the girls in town, including Taylor, Frank's granddaughter, had at one time or another studied at the Miss Denise School of Dance.

Frank had googled "yoga." Most of the related terms were Indian too, with roots in Sanskrit of course (he remembering the Hare Krishnas he'd seen in airports selling flowers, wondering wither they'd gone—regretting meanwhile getting that song, "Hare Krishna, Krishna...," stuck in his head.).

That it's an ancient practice goes without saying. There were so many forms of practice that initially he couldn't identify Dang's, but our Frank enjoys history, and also just the idea of practice. The presence of different styles like different denominations was itself interesting (a Congregationalist, he now numbered himself among the Catholics, too—a priest having been among the first to reach out to him following the unexpected death of his son, which precipitated, in order to be near Taylor, the departure from West Virginia.)

He had felt self-conscious invading Taylor's ballet space—she having expressed predictable middle school embarrassment. Maggie (whom he still considered his daughter-in- law), had inquired about the whereabouts of her daughter's pink stretching mat.

"Pink?" Big Mike joked. We were playing cards.

But Frank was seeking some sort of outlet, something untried. If he thought about it, yoga was the first new thing he'd done in quite some time, other than move to California.

The dance studio was in Old Town, in a nice 50s brick structure, Old Town having become so popular that Miss Denise acknowledged her rent had recently doubled, and had considered moving elsewhere, but in the end would find a way to make it work. A small town girl from Kansas, she'd begun as a Clippers cheerleader, married into the family that owned the franchise, divorced, and opened the studio with money from the divorce. She was, like most dancers, rather small; she had blue-black hair—shiny as a policeman's uniform; and, naturally, was in good shape. Maybe was fifty. And had had quite an interesting life—having for one thing traveled all over the world on USO missions with the intrepid Bob Hope. She worked hard at the studio and was devoted to the kids, Frank admiring her from afar.

He was, the second Friday, to again arrive early, and to sit in his truck as Dang, wearing capris-length britches and an active-wear top, opened. It was May, but we were experiencing June gloom and bloom—some mornings you could take the sky for an ocean. By the time Frank entered, Dang was already about (on quiet feet), making preparations (setting out blocks, etc.). He'd spoken to both her and Miss Denise after the first session, Dang saying that she'd emphasized strength-training not "the flowy stuff" (for his benefit?), all the while an intent, steady (almost Hare-Krishna) gleam in her eyes, both generous and nonplussed, not changing even when he mentioned that against his better judgment he sometimes still played basketball.

"Generally just shoot around by myself. Unless I get talked into a game."

"My dad says pretty much the same thing. You go to the open gym?"

"Sundays? No, mam. But if I did, I wouldn't mind schooling the kids." Frank half believing he still could.

Weirdly, he'd also felt at that moment that he and Dang had had just that conversation before.

"But when and where that possibly could have been beats me."

Apparently, Frank increasingly experienced deja vu's—even beginning as a result to question his own memory. He thought maybe these deja vu's were somehow tied to his move to another state. Were an attempt to make the strange more familiar. Or maybe they were a matter of having had held back certain feelings. He was missing his native state: rivers, fresh kale, being able to root for the Mountaineers, freedom to smoke, and, on some level mosquitoes, even ticks (his mother having once burned a tick from his skull with a match.)

"Deja vu" is French of course, but to him it had an Oriental feel to it (Sanskrit, in any case, the mother of all Indo-European languages), not that he believed in the concept of relived experiences. Likely, no such conversation with Dang had previously taken place, and even if it had, her aim, in not calling attention to the repetition, may have been simple politeness—a default position when dealing with the old.

"I can visualize my last game," Frank conceded to her.

(He'd said to Miss Denise, at Starbucks: "I think my basketball career is over," she saying, "I think so." Frank quickly covering, "Long ago," so as not to appear completely incognizant of his advancing age.)

Denise had casually rested her hand on his shoulder, like an Indian maid, at the end of the first yoga session—his having noticed previously that she would touch people in a reassuring, calming manner.

"You did good, Frank."

"Thanks. I survived."

He meant it. The stretching was indeed strenuous, especially when you also had to try and coordinate breathing, inhaling through the nose and, often, blowing out through the mouth.

"I am so weak," Miss Denise was to suddenly blurt out.

Frank saw she was embarrassed. But he hadn't noticed her struggling and certainly not so in comparison to him (he'd taken periodic breaks, astonished at the gazelle-like strength and flexibility of the women).

"Sore?" Dang was asking him now.

"A little."

(Joking to us: "I didn't want to mention my hips.")

Dang had rolled out her mat, parallel to the front mirror. There were three mirrors, and in the dim meditative light they looked like panels of gray sky. His mat took on a penis purple color. Almost fluorescent.

The room was smallish, the big practice room being behind the sliding curtain. Etiquette—he'd read up—dictated that you came to class clean, modestly dressed, with a clean mat, a towel, and your own water bottle (his blue), and, if you were a man, you were not to lurk in the back with a view of everything. He unrolled his mat in the same spot, or nearly so, as he had done the first session, not really knowing the etiquette of that though. Was it like in a school classroom, people generally taking the same seat each time? Of course he could have avoided the question altogether should he not have been, like an overanxious schoolboy, the first one there.

A couple of Asian women in their thirties had arrived, Frank saying good morning and then watching to see if they took the same spots as they had the previous week. They did. He was learning (before moving to Cali, he'd never seen anyone carrying a rolled-up yoga mat).

He described to us the "Happy Baby" position.

"You're on your back and your legs are overhead and you grab your ankles and rock gently back and forth."

Frank is a tall fellow, with a certain Southern reserve, or graciousness, so it wasn't easy but was funny to picture him doing the "Happy Baby." The thought of the happy baby position had actually brought happy memories to Frank.

Privately he admitted to a certain amount of performance anxiety. Would he improve? Would he be able to follow along? Was his mind still sharp? Too, a memory of an incident from summer was to suddenly reappear: how he'd taken Taylor and a friend of hers to the beach, and Taylor, boogie-boarding, had drifted out too far, and how he'd waded in the water and waved for her to come in, and when she didn't he was to think she was just not cooperating. In actuality the undertow was getting her, the waves were crashing loudly, like the roar of a plane, and he was unable to hear what she was saying. He hadn't spent much time around an ocean (people don't understand the force of water). Two boys, each holding one hand, brought her in, Taylor persisting long after in believing that he just hadn't wanted to wade deeper into the water.

He feared, as well, that a woman or two might decide not to take the yoga class because of him, thus bringing harm to Dang's business interests. (Commerce– exchange– at the heart of the American experience–yoga itself he thought of as a form of commerce.) In addition to teaching yoga, Dang was a part-time dance instructor at the studio, while pursuing a secondary teaching credential. (At Starbucks they'd only discussed her college studies and yoga he was pretty sure.) Whatever the effect of his presence, she had been welcoming. Yet at that moment yoga was having the opposite of a calming effect on him, perhaps the source California itself, the constant pressure to change and improve and move on it invites–necessitating yoga in effect.

"Miss Denise is running late," Dang relayed. She was generally in the habit of referring to her boss in that manner; she herself, to the dance students, was "Miss Dang." When Frank thought of Denise he too silently put "Miss." Not the case when he thought of Dang.

The brother, who'd arrived separate from his sister, looked a great deal like her. Frank was happy to no longer be the lone man. That day the brother wore black, loose-fitting yoga pants. Asian men often have a feminine quality, like European men, we generally agreed, Dang's brother of small stature. Frank had again wore long basketball shorts. Gray. Adidas. His knees looked like they'd been attacked by flesh-eating bacteria. While his thighs quivered in the mirror like jellyfish. He couldn't recall if he'd met the brother before. Maybe at one of the dance recitals. The three recitals he'd attended beginning to blur into one.

Miss Denise, her body language expressing contrition, had slipped in the back just before the commencement of the class, in a spot directly behind him. He would see her this time only in the mirror—or during warrior positions, his view of Dang unobstructed. The salutations began with the child posture, with legs bent underneath, arms out before one, followed by a walking out of the fingers forward in order to stretch out the arms and upper body, head meanwhile fallen forward resting on the mat. Next came a rising up to downward-facing-dog, through to upward- facing dog. The group—they were just seven—moved on to "the stranded beetle," Frank admitting that as far as he could tell it was the same as "happy baby." When workable he watched himself in the front mirror, in that Kodachrome light, to see if he was now reasonably in tune with the others and not in a completely different pose.

The name of the practice it turned out was Power Vinyasa, the focus on sun salutations, hip openers, twists, balancing postures, and inversions. "Inversions," he was still in the dark about. At times he found the need to take a break, while others continued. It somehow made sense to Frank that yuppies would feel the need to punish themselves. Dang however seemed to do everything effortlessly, as if the sequence were really a single extended movement (or metaphor). Miss Denise had a certain power to her movements, a strong base. When he looked at her in the mirror he imagined a young farm girl milking cows, in another posture she was chopping wood, then swimming in a river.

At last they were to rest on their backs.

"It could have been a morgue," Frank mused.

"Don't monitor your breathing now. Just let it go," Dang had said. "Let it all go. Let it find its own rhythm."

Finally, and slowly at different intervals, like patrons in a theater, post movie, the devotees rose to their feet, rolling up their mats, taking hold of their cell phones. The Asian women sipped water.

"Enjoy the weekend," Dang said.

"Enjoy Mother's Day, Miss Denise," Frank says he heard Dang say quietly just as the other women were departing (not all were mothers, probably, and Dang presumably wanted to be inclusive). He was surprised by the revelation. There was no reason for us to think Miss Denise wasn't a mother, but none of us had ever seen a child of hers around (not to mention she carried around the little black dog), though certainly her child or children would likely be on their own by now. Had we thought of Miss Denise as a kind of den mother? Had we taken the "Miss" wrong?

Mother's Day at that moment did not bring such happy memories to Frank. His Ex lived abroad now–her way of dealing with their son's death, I surmised. Frank had ceased missing her some time ago, he said.

"Yes, Happy Mother's Day, Denise," Frank chimed in nonetheless, when he and Denise reached the doorway.

"Thank you, Frank," Denise responding, her hand again on his shoulder.

Outside again, he was to look at his mat, rolled up now in the back of his truck, a part of him, maybe half he now confessed, wanting to just get in the truck and drive back east.

But Miss Denise suddenly was to appear there next to him again, still sweaty, and his hopes were raised. He didn't believe whatever he might have with Denise would match what he'd experienced in his youth–before the advent of motherhood and children, and yoga–when he and the girl used to rip each other's clothes off, when they would just hop in the truck and head out on the road together, somewhere, anywhere. It wouldn't be like that even if it were something else. But that didn't mean it wouldn't beworthwhile.

"Taylor is doing so well in dance," she said. "You should be proud."

Frank admitted, but only to me, to feeling let down. He'd been of a mind there for a minute that she'd come outside to say something different. She'd previously mentioned Taylor's development. Or at least he thought she had. Of course, Denise was maybe telling him that something might develop between the two of them if he kept coming back to yoga. But as to that he felt he had no way of knowing.

"Thank you," he was to say to Miss Denise, we understand.

Frank still had Taylor, and of course also Maggie. It might not be enough, but then again it would have to be.

After all, what had Dang said when they all put their hands together before their chest in the heart position, *angali*?

"Let us remember to express compassion and gratitude. Become aware of your breath again."

The Visit

THE FIRST PERSON I met up with was Blaine. He'd dropped out of Purdue and was working as a teller at Lafayette National, this, despite the fact that his father was the team doctor for Purdue sports teams—I'd once played golf with Blaine and his dad and Ara Parseghian, an Armenian-American, the coach of Notre Dame football at the time. I was only fourteen or so but good at golf. One oddity growing up was that Blaine's mother wasn't around, and when I thought of Blaine that was the first thing to come to mind. That, and golf. He didn't have any brothers or sisters so he lived alone with his dad. Maybe the mother had died, divorce being pretty much unheard of back then. I can't recall now so many years later. I don't know if I knew the real story at the time of my visit in '71. She was, in any case, not in the picture.

"After work we'll get the group together," he said. I was not only surprised to find him there, but also to see a male working the teller window. I didn't know anyone our age either— nineteen—who worked nine to five. I'd stopped in to cash a traveler's check. "I'm off at five," said Blaine.

"Great," I said.

He looked out at the parking lot. "Is that Mustang yours, Jack?"

The car was a "Driveway." I'd done it a couple of times before, delivered cars to people, saw Utah, New Mexico, and Texas that way. The company hired mostly young people like myself, who were free to travel. But this current deal was a private one. A man at theScottsdale country club I parked cars at—weekends while I was in college—wanted me to drop it off in a Chicago suburb, the car a birthday present for his sixteen-year-old grandson. One lucky kid was my thinking. It was a red '69 hardtop with only ten thousand miles on it—I'd checked—probably only driven to the club andback.

"I could hire a company to do it for that price," the man had said, when I asked for $75 (plus gas) not just the $50 he offered. He looked at me half-admiringly, I think. We Scots are frugal.

I didn't tell the Scotsman about my travel plans, but maybe it wouldn't have surprised him any. I'd figured if I drove pretty much straight through I'd have a couple of days in West Lafayette. Who knew when I'd have the opportunity again.

"I'll see you tonight," I told Blaine. "I might stop by Lindstrom's house."

Rick Lindstrom (he'd become "Rick" just as had Ricky Nelson)—was my best friend in elementary school.

I remember thinking, around Kansas—it was July and the alfalfa was green as jade—that I missed the Midwest. They say smells more than any other sense take you back. For me, it was irrigated farmland, cut grass, sweet-smelling lumber. My dad always liked going to the lumber yard. Midwesterners are friendly. And simple. Or at least they were back then. When they talked about the weather, they were pretty much talking about the weather.

When I thought about Rick I thought first about his crewcut. And the model airplanes he made. But by the time we were about to move west, after my sophomore year, we weren't that close—I'd switched to a more intellectual bunch, Meserle, for example (he went on to Harvard), and Steve Stein (Jewish), but Lindstrom was the first person to come to mind when I thought about a place to stay since I'd spent so many nights at his parents' house during my childhood. Rick was home from Ball State, I'd heard from Blaine. I thought of Mike Fitzgerald's, too, as a place to stay. Mike was an especially nice guy, but whenever I thought of him I also thought of his family's asphalt company which paved all the roads—I remember that smell—on both sides of town. West Lafayette was the university town and Greater Lafayette where downtown was.

Outside the bank I picked up a copy of the local paper, *The Journal and Courier*—thinking, I'll admit it, about Holly Scott when I did so. Her father owned the newspaper.

I couldn't remember if the paper was conservative—I'd recently turned more political, was in fact majoring in Political Science. *The Indianapolis Star*, which we'd get on Sundays back then, was conservative—as was *The Arizona Republic*. This was no coincidence, it turned out, since the same family, the Pulliams, owned both papers, those two papers their only holdings. Those were pretty much the two major papers I read growing up—my dad okay with that, I'm sure, he an Ohio Republican (Mom a Democrat, and a New Yorker). Come to think of it Dad probably choose conservative Arizona for its politics, among other things. Before that, he'd considered accepting a job at Georgia Tech and I couldn't help but wonder how different my life would have been were that to have had happened.

Holly was never my girlfriend. More like a protective older sister than anything else. I had all brothers. She was Johnny Raymond's girlfriend. Johnny, too, had taken me under his wing. They were seniors when I was a sophomore. But I hadn't forgotten the summer night Holly told me—I'd come over to say goodbye and we were chatting outside her bedroom window—that if it happened that she wasn't with Johnny for some reason she would have wanted to be with me, wanted me for a boyfriend. She smiled, her green eyes like cat's eyes, like marbles. I didn't take it to mean there was anything lacking in her relationship with Johnny, and I knew even back then that she was telling me what she was telling me due my moving away—giving me maybe something to take with me, if doing so from a safe distance—but if you'd known Holly Scott back then you'd understand how much it meant to me. Her being older to boot. It was funny to think that she may have been thinking what she was, about me, even when she was with Johnny, even when I talked to them at school. Girls have such thoughts, too, I was learning. We'd sat in the dewy grass together. She wore only a nightee and was barefoot. The sky was blanketed with stars, the way it is in rural places. It was memorable.

"Look, Jack," she said, "you can see the big dipper."

I gave her a photo album that summer night, with a school picture of myself inside. My mom found it sort of amusing that I would do that. I guess it was not something to do, especially when you were headed elsewhere. I remember a friend had made fun of me for saying "Good luck to you, too" when Tommy Morrissey's dad had wished us bon voyage and good luck. But if Holly thought it was amusing, she didn't let on. I wasn't expecting to see her this time around, but I couldn't help but wonder what had become of her, whether she were still in town, still with Johnny or not, and maybe if she still had that picture.

"Is that your car?" Mrs. Lindstrom asked, too.

She said Rick was over at Barb Kuntz's house, the Kuntzs' house being right next to the Fitzgerald's. The Kuntzs always had a Cadillac and the Mike's family an Imperial, the two cars parallel to each other in their respective driveways. Mike—we called him "Mic"—got upset at me one time when I suggested Cadillacs had a better ride. Meserle thought I'd said Catholics. You remember those sorts of things. Mike and Meserle were both Catholic. Morrissey, too. Meserle and I had built a Soapbox Derby car together, he doing most of the engineering although my dad was the engineering professor.

Mrs. L and I were in the kitchen. Their kitchen, unlike ours back then, had a countertop between it and the dining room. Made of laminate, I guess. There is nothing so strange as going, as a child, to a friend's house for the first time. Especially a best friend. To see how different each of us lives. There were only three Lindstrom kids. Judy, the eldest, was the brainy one. Rick the youngest of the three. The house had a modern feel unlike ours—things matched. It had what I now take as a mid-century modern look, clean, sleek, efficient. The red bar stools hadn't changed. Nor had Mrs. L's coifed hair, though now it wasn't Swedish blond but gray.

"No, Mrs. Lindstrom, I'm delivering the car to someone in Chicago," I'd answered. "It's supposed to be there by Sunday."

We sat then at the kitchen table. It was a warm, humid day. She'd got me some ice tea with ginger ale in it to drink.

"I wish I could offer for you to stay here, Jack," she said, "it would be fun to see you and Rick together—we still have the double beds in that room. But maybe you heard Mr. Lindstrom is paralyzed and confined to his bed and I think it might be awkward for you."

"I'm sorry to hear that. I hadn't heard."

"He's asleep right now."

"No problem. Mike Fitzgerald has already offered," I lied. "I always liked coming here though. I always felt welcome, Mrs. Lindstrom," I added. I didn't know quite how to respond to the news about Mr. L. He'd always been nice to me. He was a quiet guy. When I thought of him, I thought of his profession. He made false teeth.

Boys had sleepovers in our town. When I mention this, people are in some cases surprised. In their town only girls had sleepovers. Sometimes we scheduled a slumber party to coincide with the girl's slumber party. And then raid it. But I don't think we ever surprised them much. I think they expected it, waited for it.

"It's hard to get good help these days," Mrs. Lindstrom was saying, in reference to taking care of her husband.

I suppose that was how it happened that Mrs. L and I entered into a political discussion. We were waiting for Rick–she'd called over to the Kuntz house. All I remember is that we got onto the topic of race, she saying that Negroes work too slowly, that they lack a work ethic. I'd never thought of her politics.

"Black people do a lot of the tough jobs," I countered. "They drive buses, pick up trash, work assembly lines. Serve in the military. And other things. They keep the world running."

It was weird to have an adult conversation like that with Rick's mom, but I was thinking if I was going to be political I had to speak up.

I was glad Rick came in just then though. And I was glad to see him (a few years later I would see him walking along Mill Avenue in Tempe and I wouldn't even hail him down. Maybe he saw me, too, I don't know. He was stationed at the Air Force base, I'd heard.)

At the time he'd lost the crewcut he'd sported as a kid.

"We're going to the Boilermaker, Mom," he said. "Jack, I got in touch with Dobson, Rags, Mic of course. Morrissey. Bill Blaine, as you know."

"Great. Thanks, Rick," I said.

The drinking age was eighteen.

I said goodbye to Mrs. Lindstrom. Her son's hospitality was like hers. Many times they had invited me to their cottage on Lake Freeman. I learned to ski there, Mr. L captaining the speed boat. At first it's hard to figure how to pull yourself out of the water. The idea is to let the rope do the work. They were very patient with me, circling back around again and again. Once you're up though you never forget how, like riding a bike. Another memory is of Mr. L sitting alone at the end of the pier fishing.

Nor can I forget how on the way to the lake we'd always stopped in for chocolate enclairs and on the way home, usually a Sunday afternoon, we'd stop by the lemon custard stand.

It was shocking to learn they belonged to the John Birch Society. My father was conservative, but he was never a Bircher. There was a big chapter in Indiana.

Not to this day do I quite understood the JBS campaign against fluoride in drinking water.

The Boilermaker was a block from campus. The campus was all red brick and so was the Boilermaker. It was a kind of incipient sports bar. Only Rags hadn't made it. But Jill had, unexpectedly. And Alexandra Van Natter, who was now Morrissey's wife. For a while I'd dated Charlotte, her identical twin, but Charlie had broke up with me and gone back to Blaine. Sitting there across from Alex–the table was made out of logs and there was sawdust on the floor–I could more than imagine what Charlie now looked like, too. Alex was as cute as ever. She had red hair, they both did. Her looks would help balance out Morrissey's when they had a kid, I was thinking. He wasn't a bad-looking guy, but he had big ears.

I can't say it was fate that Jill was there. I knew she had been close to Holly, despite the two-year age difference. Jill was sort of fast, that might explain it. She didn't seem to have much interest in boys her own age. I remembered seeing her with Holly sometimes, Jill dark-haired and Holly blond. I think she even double-dated with Holly and Johnny a time or two. I know they had. With Finkelstein, I think.

I worked to get a seat next to Jill. It may have looked like I was trying to hit on her–no one would have been surprised by that–but I guessed that Jill was aware of my real motives. She had in front of her a whiskey with a beer chaser, a boilermaker, the local speciality. I was sticking to just beer, feeling that all the driving had caught up with me a little. I'd done about five hundred miles a day.

It was odd to all drink together. We'd done some drinking at sixteen–although not a lot–but it was weird to be in a real establishment drinking, just like the college kids we'd always looked up to, who we now were. I was thinking back on how summer of fifth grade a few of us had hung out at the empty SAE fraternity house, the students gone home. Most days we would steal a pack of cigarettes from Arth's Drug store and then would loll around the frat house, smoking, and reading left behind Playboys. (Later I would tell people that I gave up smoking in fifth grade.)

We'd ordered a pitcher of Bud and a pitcher of Coors, Coors suddenly very popular.

"It was more fun when you were here," Morrissey said.

"Yeah," Dobson agreed. He was home from Depauw.

"Thanks. But I think maybe I was pretty full of myself then."

"I didn't think so," Morrissey said.

"Well, a little," Alex chimed in.

We all laughed. It was just a great feeling.

It was then I asked about Charlie trying not to catch Blaine's eye. And after all, it was almost ancient history. I learned she was at I.U. and wasn't coming home for the summer. "P.U." (our rival's designation) and I.U. were the primary choices, Purdue more for Engineering and Indiana more for Liberal Arts. Had we stayed in Indiana I would have probably gone to I.U. But you can't reimagine your life. Once the blanks have been filled in you can't go back and imagine another destiny. Only faulty memory allows any room for improvisation.

"Holly heard you're here," Jill whispered in my ear, maybe giving the impression she was trying to pick *me* up.

I whispered back. "Is she still with Johnny?"

"He's in Vietnam. She'd like to see you before you leave town."

Somehow our majors had come up. Mike was a business major. When I'd known Mic in high school he'd wanted to become a physical therapist. He was the team trainer for the high school basketball team—which I'd played on. He took care of me and the others when we twisted an ankle or something. But now he was working over the summer in the family street-paving business and was being groomed to take over once he finished college.

"Political science," I said. "I was telling Rick's mom this afternoon that I felt like I was I was the only one who supported Kennedy back then."

The assassination was something we'd all gone through together in junior high. I was remembering, too, how my Ohio grandma didn't have a good word for President Kennedy until he was killed.

"My family was for Kennedy," Morrissey inserted. "But we kept quiet about it."

"It's not so conservative here now," Dobson said.

"Yes it is," Rick put in.

"Well, still pretty conservative," Dobson laughed.

Jill was smiling. Maybe Holly had told her everything. I hated to think what Holly had told me privately was public knowledge in any respect. But I at least knew that Holly hadn't entirely forgotten me.

Jill had finished her whiskey and threw back her beer.

I turned to the group, my friends. The kids I'd grown up with. And had gone to school with, starting in kindergarten.

I told them how I'd delivered *The Journal and Courier* for three months one summer and I was wondering the other day what happened to that route (not pronounced "root") after I'd dropped it and how my younger brother said he carried it on for two more years, Mom often driving him around when it was rainy or snowy.

"How can you forget so soon something thathappened only a few years earlier?" I said, raising my glass wobbly-like.

Everyone laughed at that, too.

"Weren't you always a Tenderfoot?" Dobson said.

"Yeah, I didn't earn a single merit badge in boy scouts. I was only interested in the outings. But in choosing the intrepid Rick here as my tent mate, I chose well. I used to stay in the tent until I could smell breakfast. I'd raise myself up from my sleeping bag and peer through the flap—yep, there was Rick, kneeling before the campfire."

"Self-reliance!" Rick joked.

I sipped my beer. Feeling actually woozy at that point.

"I hate to call it quits so early," I said.

Mic looked at me. "You sure you want to do that?"

I don't know what he knew.

Jill offered to drive me. She seemed somehow invested in my seeing Holly. Maybe it was just out of her friendship for Holly, or maybe she knew that Holly was lonely with Johnny gone.

"You don't want to crash that car before it's delivered," she said.

I'd forgotten all about the car and my mission to deliver it.

I told Mic I'd be over later. He had his own place out near Lafayette Country Club. At one point I'd begged my mom for golf lessons so I could compete with the country club kids. She got me a month's worth of lessons at the club, but the professional wanted to completely change my swing. Make it more inside out.

When Jill and I were in her car—a Chevelle—I asked what I'd wanted to ask much earlier.

"Are they married, Jill?"

"Not until he gets back. Her father won't allow it."

"You mean, just as friends she wants to see me?"

"It's not up to me."

Jill laughed. She seemed to realize her non sequitur.

"I couldn't do that."

"What?"

"I'm opposed to the war."

We were stopped at a light on Meridian near the high school. Searchlights atop the school shone across the football field, the dark bleachers on each side. When I thought about Johnny Raymond, I recalled how he'd set up metal chairs in his backyard and practice his moves, his jukes and cutbacks, running through that line of chairs.

The light changed and we headed up the hill.

"She's at her house, Jack. She's living at home until Johnny gets back."

"I don't know. Don't you feel funny delivering me?"

"A little. But her parents aren't home. They're on vacation."

"Are they for the war? Is the paper pro-war?"

"How would I know. I guess they are, it is. This isn't Madison or Berkeley, Jack. You know, you've changed. I don't remember you as having any qualms."

Holly had turned twenty-one just the week earlier—I remembered her birthday. I kept quiet about the fact that I'd been married, in high school, and had a kid. Having a son had kept me out of the war; I was III-A. Blaine, too, I learned later—that's why he was working nine-to-five. He'd gotten Charlie pregnant.

Once I'd divorced I was to lose that deferment. But my lottery number was high enough that I was still safe.

"You know, Horse was killed last year. And Bradshaw," Jill said. "No one mentioned it?"

"Oh, my god, Horse. And Brads. I'm so sorry to hear that."

Horse and Brads and Johnny Raymond and many others as it turned out.

Skid Row, Venice

A STARBUCKS OFF Venice Beach, late morning. Light filters in from a window. Sitting at adjoining tables are Jeremiah, twenty-five, and Linda, forty. The tables form a right angle facing the audience. He has a venti-size coffee in front of him, which he nurses, and she a tall coffee in front of her. He is tall and thin. His hair is cut short. He wears a bright tie-dye shirt, torn blue jeans, and sandals. He's sunburned. A big blue travel bag sits on the seat next to him. She looks fifty or more. But is now sober. She is dressed like a forlorn prep school girl, high socks and all. Her cell phone is on her table.

LINDA

I like your shirt.

(He glances up shyly.)

JEREMIAH

Thank you.

LINDA

How much did it cost?

JEREMIAH

Thirty dollars. I bought it the day I arrived here.

LINDA

How long ago was that?

(He sips his coffee.)

JEREMIAH

About two weeks. My grandma died.

LINDA

My condolences. I'm sure you miss her.

JEREMIAH

She was very religious.

(She reaches out her hand to shake. They shake.)

Nice to meet you.

LINDA

I used to live here, on the beach. But now I have an apartment. I live in Koreatown. My mother used to give me twenty dollars a day when I lived down here. But then I got sober. I still would get the twenty dollars. ...Were you in the military?

JEREMIAH

Yes, I was. Two years.

LINDA

I did three years of college. ...Do you have any money?

JEREMIAH

No, Mam, I don't.

(She hands him a five-dollar bill. He
looks at it carefully.)

I appreciate it. I'm related to Lincoln—he's my third cousin or something like that. Money is symbolic. It's power, and respect.

LINDA

Where are you from?

JEREMIAH

Illinois.

(She sips her coffee. Then reaches out
her hand.)

LINDA

I'm Linda.

(Bemused, he shakes again.)

JEREMIAH

Jeremiah.

LINDA

Lincoln is an institution now but suffered from depression. ...I read a lot of books now. It's important to find other activities. Mindfulness, too. Meditation. I'm happy I got off the beach. A lot of partying on the beach. I slept on the sand, on streets, in shopping carts. Do you know where Rose and Lincoln is—the street Lincoln?

JEREMIAH

Yes.

LINDA

You can get a free meal there. A shower. Wash your clothes. St. Joseph's is good, too. They have nurses and doctors.

JEREMIAH

I'm disease free, healthy as an ox. I get checked out.

LINDA

Good. My sponsor has AIDS and Hep C.

JEREMIAH

He does?

LINDA

She does. She may not survive. I might lose her.

JEREMIAH (abstractedly, as if speaking to someone in his past)

I'm sorry.

(Then Jeremiah, as if returning to familiar things, and pointing to his head.)

I've got ESP. You heard of it? I'm a powerful detective—but right now I'm taking a break. I could be of help to the LAPD if they have a hard case. But I'm letting my mind cool down, I'm too stressed.

LINDA

Yes, it gets like that.

JEREMIAH

But love can change that.

LINDA

Yes, love is a powerful thing.

JEREMIAH (suddenly near tears)

Love is a beautiful thing. Beautiful as high corn.

LINDA (nodding)

You said it better than I did.

(Jeremiah sips his coffee.)

JEREMIAH

I know how to love, you can see it in my eyes.

LINDA (sincerely)

Yes, I can.

JEREMIAH (matter of factly)

I have a very, very strong mind. I can tell when people mean it and when they don't. I'm glad God gave me that power.

LINDA

How can you?

JEREMIAH (tinged with anger)

I can tell, that's all.

LINDA (soothingly)

I care about you. You have people who care about you.

JEREMIAH

Oh, I know that. I'm appreciative, Mam. ...I'm not a bad guy, I'm not crazy.

(He shakes his empty coffee cup.)

LINDA

Refills are fifty cents here. But there's no restroom. Too many people coming in off the street. Or tourists. It is a beautiful beach. White as cocaine.

(She sips her coffee.)

Have you heard of neuroplasticity?

JEREMIAH

Don't believe so.

LINDA

The brain is a living thing. Not static. It changes as you change. If you do one thing for a long time—like drink or whatever—you build synapses that need that pleasure. But if you do other things, you build up, over time, different synapses. Different areas of pleasure.

(There is a pause as Jeremiah takes this in and thinks of a way to respond.)

JEREMIAH

I wouldn't want to lose my power. My grandma tried to take it away.

(They sit quietly. He pulls his phone out of his pants, pulls earbuds from his travel bag, and, off his phone, listens to music. She sits observing him for a minute. Then picks up her phone and looks at it.)

LINDA (abstractedly)

Of course there are environmental factors. It makes me think of the canals.

JEREMIAH (removing his earbuds)

Did you say something, Linda?

LINDA

I was wondering if you've seen the canals? Just like Venice, Italy.

JEREMIAH

I've heard of them.

LINDA

They're like a latticework of water. It's easy to get lost.

JEREMIAH

I'd like to see them sometime. I've got a natural curiosity about things.

LINDA (flatly)

I need to catch the bus. I live in Koreatown. My mother used to give me twenty dollars a day when I lived down here.

JEREMIAH

Yes, you mentioned that.

LINDA

Did I?

JEREMIAH

Yes, but it's okay.

LINDA

Then I got sober. I've been sober two years. Once you've been sober for a year you're free to talk about it. Do you know where the mental health center is?

JEREMIAH

I know one of them. Down the block.

LINDA

I could show you a better one. Not that I'm being critical. There are people around who genuinely want to help. Ex-cons, anyone in need.

JEREMIAH (aggressively)

I'm not about to tell them anything.

LINDA

No, of course you don't have to.

(She puts her phone in her pocket. He holds his. Then, half to herself...)

Only if you want to.

(They remain seated for a moment more.)

Shall we go?

(They rise together, leaving their coffee cups. Wander off stage side-by-side— a Mutt and Jeff—but as if they are not together.)

Beginnings

DONNA, MY STUDENT, wasn't free after Psych class the Thursday following the ash storm—our first encounter had included among other things a Santa Ana fire, the silent ash sifting through the air, the barbeque pink and gray horizon visible through the eucalyptus stand outside the VA grounds. But she was free the following week. We returned to our spot overlooking the Valley. It was the clearest of evenings, and had its own kind of magic—though I suppose anytime you fall for someone the beginning is magical. Donna had commented over the phone one night about how much she liked "beginnings."

The phone seems to me a false magic, but Donna felt otherwise. She liked to talk on the phone—to rehearse the day's events—so we talked. She did all of the calling—in fact, her phone number was blocked. She would call when out doing errands. I'd hear the crunching of her feet when she walked, or background noises. And sometimes her boy, Jeremiah, was with her. She'd speak Spanish to him or to someone waiting on them. Sometimes she'd even call from home when her husband was there. She liked talking, and admittedly often I enjoyed the conversation, too.

I was piecing together her background. She was twenty-two and worked as a surgical tech at the hospital. Born in Texas, she'd grown up in East L.A. with a single mother and an older brother and sister. Although Mexican on her mother's side—Donna had nut-brown hair, a small broad nose, dark eyes—she'd been raised Jehovah Witness. Her father was Irish. And he drank. She'd only recently reestablished contact. Her brother was in jail for carjacking but was trying to get transferred to a psychiatric facility to reduce his time. "Perhaps you could help," she'd said to me. Her older sister was married and still a Witness. Donna's seven-year-old lived with her ex- husband during the week and with her on weekends, so that she could further her education. "Maybe I'm just not cut out to be a full-time mom," she'd admitted. She left her son's father to be with a thirty-seven-year-old, Jewish doctor. She was sixteen then. They were together for three years. Then she lived alone, with her son, for two years. Six months before we'd met, she married for a second time, to Carlos, an El Salvadorian. He was forty-one, the same age as her father. He'd been a Navy Seal. I myself was forty-five.

"I like talking to you, Henry," she said as we looked out at the Valley lights. "You're a good teacher, you know so much. At work the doctors make fun of me. The other day one said: 'Donna, what's the purple animal figure on tv that kids like?' 'Barney,' I said. 'Right,' he said, 'that's what Donna knows!' All docs are assholes."

"I beg your pardon."

"Not that they don't want to work with me—breathe in a little youth, you know."

"Especially as they can't see much of you underneath those scrubs," I said.

Then we were quiet. I hadn't kissed Donna, but I was working up to it. It was up to me to press for physical contact and for her to set boundaries, especially as she was the one who was married. I'd been, like the Jewish doctor, through a messy divorce.

She'd recently heard, via e-mail, from him. He'd set up his own practice, in West L.A., and wanted her to run his office because he knew, she said, that he could trust her. "Sounds like he wants you back," I'd said to this.

Thinking of him, I said: "Wasn't he worried about seeing a sixteen-year-old girl?"

"I think he was sometimes."

"I went out with a student who turned out to be sixteen. But I didn't know it at first."

"At first?"

"Well, not right at first," I laughed.

"How far did it go?"

Donna shifted in her seat, leaned across the console. The real magic is that people who need each other find each other.

"Well, we didn't have intercourse, thank god," I whispered.

"What did you do?"

I could tell that she wanted me to talk about it.

"Well..."

"Cat got your tongue. Do you want me to say it for you? Did you like her soft skin?"

"It was good for my ego."

"And?"

"That's when I found out she was sixteen. She shouldn't have been in college."

Donna laughed.

I went in to kiss her and she let me hold her hand. We hugged tight. I'd almost forgotten what a girl's breasts feel like when pressing up against you. Though sometimes I hug my brother's wife, Tina.

I tried to break the clinch so I could look at Donna and try to kiss her again or at least kiss her neck. But she held on tight. She was crying. Then we kissed madly, I was all inside her wide, supple mouth. I felt the tears as they ran off her nose. I held her slim fingers. And then touched the top of her ass. I buried my face in her soft, thick hair.

"Why are you crying?" I whispered.

"My sister's wedding is today," she said.

I tried for more. "Can I touch your breasts?" I said, awkwardly, and then reached for her.

"No," she said. "I'm sorry. Guess it's my upbringing. We were hammered about fornication. There was all the talk about the end of the world and damnation." She added: "I wasn't invited to her wedding."

Donna was aware of her propensities, for drama generally and older men specifically, and saw in them not only higher self-actualization factors but also lower, yet crucial, pyramid needs for love and affection.

"The absent father," I said. We were on the phone again.

"I can't deny it," Donna laughed. "But I like you, Henry. I don't know what it is. There's something between us, isn't there. Do you know what it is? It's true that you look like my father, the handsomest man I've ever met."

"I'll take that as a compliment," I said. But I was tired of talking on the phone. I wanted Donna there with me. "I never see you," I complained.

"But neither does my husband. Or my son. You're not the only one."

"Who doesn't get enough of you? Or are you alluding to other lovers?"

"How many girlfriends do you have?" she shot back.

"Are you my girlfriend? Four then," I funned.

"You know I'm busy, Henry."

So was I. My duties at the hospital–my speciality was Juvenile Schizophrenia (which I hasten to point out doesn't usually involve multiple personalities, or DID, Disassociated Identity Disorder, but rather such symptoms as anti-social behavior, hallucinations and delusions, and memory lapses)–along with my teaching, kept me busy. It was catch-as-catch-can with Donna and me.

Thanksgiving weekend she flew with Carlos, and a Salvadorian couple, to San Salvador, Donna looking forward to the trip because, as she said, she liked new places. She brought me back a present, giving it to me as we sat together, this time before class and in the botanical garden. It was a mask. Mayan.

"Quetzalcoatl," I said. "The Plumed Serpent."

"See, that's why I love you, Henry, you're so smart."

"Known also as 'Kukulcan,'" I said for good measure.

I was thinking of Donna's use of the word "love," a use we'd avoided so far.

We were on a bench, protected from the wind. Birds and squirrels squittered among the plants; as Christmas was coming, some houses on the hillside were strung with lights.

I snuck my hand underneath her text books and held her thigh while she talked.

"There's so much poverty in El Salvador," she said, explaining that they'd had a good time and the beaches were good and the other couple nice–she was the youngster in the group–but that there was garbage everywhere and poor plumbing some places and that she "wasn't a humble person." She and the others had brought discarded clothes to hand out to the poor. Taking care of those in the old country was an expectation for those who'd made a new beginning in America. "But it was good to see where Carlos was from," she continued.

Of course I didn't like hearing about Carlos and any good news about their marriage, such as the vacation, was not good news to me. On the phone one time we'd discussed their sex life, in relation to our own which had yet to have really begun.

"Are you looking forward to our sex," she'd said. "I'm going to cheat with you and then never again."

"Good," I responded, "that means you won't cheat on me."

I'd explained to Donna my desires. She said that she and David had had anal sex and she liked it. "Can you come that way?" I asked. She said yes, she could. Still, she felt it best that we take things slow. "If we started sleeping together a certain specialness would be gone," she said.

There were two weeks left in the semester. I feared the absence of teacher-student dynamics might affect us, but Donna claimed otherwise. She was supposed to return to El Salvador January first with her husband and his mother—who still owned a house there—but she had told Carlos she wasn't going and encouraged him to go without her.

He'd looked at her and said, "You know what you're doing. You know what you're doing," as though he was on to something.

"You could sleep over," I said as we walked to class, "since his mom would be gone, too."

"His brother lives around the corner," said Donna.

"It's hopeless," I whined.

"We'll see," Donna said.

L.A. was a series of ethnic conclaves; oddly, my own apartment bordered on an El Salvadorian neighborhood, as well as Koreatown, and Hancock Park. The latter was a lovely walk from my apartment through a manicured neighborhood. To Starbucks. But sometimes I'd head in the opposite direction. I would get my haircut at Mercedes a block down, and liked the taqueria for burritos, and would get my car washed—exterior only—at Miguel's. At Dunkin' Donuts I'd order the #1 combo—a small coffee and two donuts, plain cake—and would sit at one of the plastic yellow booths and just like at Starbucks would read, first the sports page, then the news, and finally, usually, in a novel. I also liked to watch the people. Those who came in were generally cheerful, gregarious, seemingly wholesome types, little kids in tow. Occasionally a bum would be slumped down over in a booth. Some may have found it odd that I would read at Dunkin' Donuts—not so at Starbucks of course—but there was a live and let live attitude which covered even the bum.

I gave Donna an "A" in the class. She'd earned it. Her work was "B+" not "A," but she worked really hard and was overcoming a lack of domain knowledge.

For Christmas, I went to Phoenix. My daughter would be there—from Maine. My parents and three of my five brothers lived in Phoenix. I had no sister.

I suppose the difference in ages, between Donna and me, was a problem. Donna once joked about telling "the moms." "My mom would cross her eyes, disbelieving. Then say: 'I want you to be happy, Donna. Whatever will make you happy.' My mom is the sweetest person in the world." Yet oddly, Donna saw her mom only two or three times a year even though she lived but fifteen minutes away, in Burbank.

Donna wasn't invited to the wedding because she was shunned. Even her dad could go because he'd never been a Witness. After their father had left them, Donna's mother took the family to live with her brothers in San Bernadino. They were all Witnesses. "I lived a deprived childhood," she'd explained. "Repressed, you might say. Boys were shooed away. My uncles wouldn't let me stand before the front window."

Carlos decided after all to accompany his mother to San Salvador that week after Christmas. Donna called minutes after dropping him and his mom off at LAX.

"Do you want me to come over?"

"Yes."

"You sound tired."

"I want you to, believe me. It's just that I'm on call. One of my patients is having an episode."

"I don't have to come."

"Donna, I want you to. I just might have to leave in medias res."

"In the middle of things."

"Right."

"I'll need directions," she said.

We didn't hesitate to cuddle in bed, in the near dark—one string of Christmas lights, which I'd hung for her, the only illumination. Donna, surprisingly shy, kept her clothes on.

"You're thin," she said, running her hand along my chest.

"Easy to operate on," I said.

"At the end of the month I'm getting my tonsils removed. The male surgical techs and nurses keep joking about how happy they'd be to assist in the room. But I won't need to be naked just fortonsils."

"Open your mouth. Let me see," I said.

"Yes, doctor."

I kissed the back of Donna's mouth. I removed her bra and kissed her breasts.

"My nipples are small, aren't they?"

"I like small nipples."

"I see women on the operating table who have these huge eye-dropper nipples."

We were both comfortable talking about bodies.

"When I first started working—I was only eighteen," Donna continued, "I was a bit shocked by all the cocks and balls I saw!"

I hovered over Donna, hard. But she kept her shorts on.

"I'm not on the pill, or anything," she said. "And we shouldn't anyway."

"You guys don't use protection?"

"Just Russian roulette," she said, not really defensive. "I'm careful. I just know I'm not going to get pregnant. I don't want to. Except maybe with you, Henry. What a beautiful child we'd have. It would be your masterpiece. A little blue-eyed boy. Or girl. I love your blue eyes."

"If you get pregnant with Carlos, any chance we have would go out the window," I responded.

I looked at the Christmas lights and suddenly felt depressed. Predictably, my beeper went off. It vibrated on the night stand.

"You know, you're not magically protected," I said to Donna, the nastiest thing I'd said to her.

"You're right," she said. "But you weren't in the picture until recently. The pill makes me fat. You said you liked anal."

I called my service.

"I'll have to go, Donna," I reported. "Want to ride with me?"

"That's protocol?"

"In an emergency,"

I joked, as I dressed.

"I'm sleepy anyway."

"You do look comfy. I won't be that long," I agreed.

I reviewed encounters with Donna as I drove to Chatsworth, where Aaron, my patient, lived. Ironically, the fire that Donna and I had witnessed was in Chatsworth. "Birthday candles," I'd joked at the time because, just to add to the magic, our first encounter happened to be on her twenty-second birthday. As a Witness, Donna hadn't celebrated birthdays.

The drive up took me through several charred acres, lit here and there with Christmas lights.

"Magical," I laughed to myself.

The episode turned out to be minor. Aaron was off his meds and his speech patterns were mixed, though he was clear enough in suggesting that his mother wanted him out of the way so she could live alone with his older brother.

"I don't want him institutionalized again, doctor," Mrs. Silver said to me.

Her face was a mask of disbelief. They were Jewish.

"That won't be necessary," I said.

I looked forward to telling Donna the whole story, about, for instance, how I'd reached Aaron by talking about his beloved Lakers. I looked forward to again having someone to share my work with. And my bed, even if only irregularly.

But Donna wasn't there when I got back. The apartment was dark except for a light in the bathroom. But she wasn't in the bathroom. I waited late into the night for her to call, but nothing. Two days passed, three. Nothing. She didn't come back to class. I had no way of contacting her directly–except through the hospital. But the hospital registry didn't show a home address. A week passed. Two. Should I track her down? I'd begun to hate her. And I felt a wound to my pride.

Things begin before you realize that they have, and they end before you realize it–to find out which was the case, was my desire. I knew what floor she worked on.

"Yes, Donna Rodriguez or O'Leary," I said to the young ward clerk. "You were friends?"

"We were, yes. Were you, doctor?"

I hesitated. Should I claim she was my patient?

"Yes."

"I think Donna quit," the girl continued. "No one knows what happened to her. She never came back after her tonsilitis."

"But you must know where she lived?"

"We were only work friends. I'm sure personnel would know."

She looked at me. As if knowing I wouldn't be contacting personnel.

Pictures

THEIR STUFF WAS stacked up, mostly in boxes, in the middle of the livingroom. Just moving was stressful enough, wasn't it? Now this interruption. This complication. He looked at the boxes, the empty book shelves, at his golf bag leaning against the recliner, the two box fans.

"What a time for this to happen," said Rich. "Fumigating, my God."

"Do you think the plant will die?"

Together they looked at the bamboo bonsai. It had retained much of its original shape. Housed in a white and blue Ming vase (which Claire pronounced like "was"), Rich had made her a present of it. Or rather, at her importuning had bought it at the farmer's market in their old neighborhood. Now they were moving again. But it was impending fumigation that resulted in them being up since five.

"I don't like thinking Debbie will sleep in an exterminated room. I don't trust what they say. Do you?"

All Rich could picture was a big pitched tent—a red and yellow one—dwarfing the whole apartment complex. But there'd be no circus under that tent, or anything else. They were to be out by eight a.m. and wouldn't be allowed back in until noon Friday. After that, they had but a week to move. Christmas week. Not ideal either. Although he did like the idea of being, by New Year's, in a new apartment, even if it was only just another apartment.

"I'll do the food if you do the toiletries," said Claire.

"They said only the things we ingest."

"And you believe them? It's gas. We are taking the bedding, too."

There was no arguing with this. The house was her prerogative, her domain. Although, as Debbie was asleep, it was an opportune, even apt time to argue.

But Rich just watched his wife walk into the kitchen. She did look good in sweats.

He walked into the bathroom.

Did she mean everything? Lipstick, shaving cream, make-up? Toothpaste, of course. It was something you ingested, even if you spit it out.

Rich was tossing everything into a bag. Plastic had been banned by the city, but the fumigators had given each household four big nylon polymer bags. Canned food, animal feed, cigarettes, even stuff in the refrigerator, including condiments, were on the list. You double- bagged everything, one bag at a time, twisting the top and securing with tape. You did this in accordance with the instructions, which showed a woman doing it.

He was sure Claire meant medicines. They were anyway also on the list, if the seal wasn't intact. Some medicines might be saved, he figured. He looked at capsule bottles. Anything past its expiration date he was tossing out. The codeine still had two weeks so he was keeping that. The case to her birth control pills was open. He hadn't looked closely at those since they were college kids. There'd been those two years when she'd gone off them and it had been the best two years of their lives. And luckily they'd gotten Debbie. Claire was ecstatic and he, too.

She leaned against the door frame, one arm propped. He liked the way she looked like that, in her exasperation. In her sweats.

"What are you doing?"

"Checking dates. Culling things."

They'd culled some books a week earlier, the public library happy to get them. Some of the books were from back when he was single.

"I don't want to shop again before our move," he continued. "But maybe we should just toss the food."

"I couldn't. I'll admit it would be easier," she said.

"At least we won't need to shop again."

"Yes. I think I remember you saying something like that."

Claire smiled. Maybe she wasn't so annoyed after all.

"Debbie's asleep," he proffered.

"Okay. Let me wash my hands."

"Me first." He elbowed her aside. "I used to fight with my sister for the bathroom." She looked at him. "I've said that before?"

It was almost as good as during those two years when she wasn't on the pill. Fast and simultaneous. Maybe they'd just been in a rut lately.

Debbie was up.

"Are we moving?"

"Not today," Claire explained.

"We're going to a motel."

"We're going to live in a motel? Forever?"

"No, honey," Rich explained. "Just for a vacation. Just two days."

"I want to live in a motel."

She looked like her mother. The same cardboard-blond hair and the more squarish face. Rich sometimes looked in vain for his own genes. But Claire said that was nonsense, Debbie had his eyes and his personality. "You can't see it because you can't see yourself." He agreed that that was a fundamental existential conundrum. Not that any of that mattered when it came to Debbie. Like any philosophy it only took you so far. Stoicism, for example. Existentialism had nothing to say about familial ties.

Some people had already left the night before. In the rain, and it was still raining. He'd watched from the front window one young woman, bent backed, moving through the porch light shadows with a big suitcase behind her. She'd only moved in the week before and Rich didn't know her. Wouldn't get to know her. What a howdy-do for her: you just move in and you have to be out for two days. He didn't suppose the rain would put a damper on the fumigation. The termites were goners, rain or no rain. It was funny to think about being surrounded by something you couldn't see, eating wood. Only whole-structure fumigation promised success, said the brochure. But Rich had argued with the management company about the timing.

"People are getting packages. People are taking final exams. Having visitors come."

"It's not up for discussion."

Claire had tugged his sleeve, so he'd let it go. They'd be out of there soon enough. But he was sure he wouldn't get all his deposit back. The Long Beach Police were out of control, too. They'd shot a guy dead who, intoxicated, pointed a garden hose at them and they claimed they thought it was a gun. They hadn't even issued a warning. The dead man, divorced, had an eight- year-old son. It was a flat-out ambush, almost a massacre. The man, out of work, had been as a youth a top swimmer at Milikan High School, maybe the highlight of his life. Hours and hours of laps in the pool, it required. The Long Beach Police just gunned him down. They'd called in ten back-up patrols because a neighbor had reported a drunk man sitting on his porch with, so the caller thought, a gun in his hand. Two-thirds of the city budget went to police and fire, while hundreds of teachers were pink-slipped.

The sky was white-gray. It was a light, almost invisible rain. Water drops reflected off the glass and appeared to be running like sperm across his desk. He was writing some checks, although he'd come into the bedroom to grab the bedding. Debbie wanted Fluffy the Bear as well as her pillow. Trix was coming too of course, however interesting it might be see if a cat could survive.

"Let's wear our hoodies," Claire said, to Debbie. They'd come into the bedroom. "We've only got half an hour."

Rich turned: "They can wait."

"Don't start something, Rich. Something you started a little while ago put us behind schedule."

"They said approximately eight, not exactly eight. I don't see them, do you? I bet they don't show until ten or so. Probably never intended to. You know how these people work. Maybe they'll call it off due to the rain."

"Don't argue, Daddy," Debbie suddenly said. "It's Christmas."

She'd never interfered before, never even suggested that she heard the disagreements.

"It's not Christmas yet," he muttered. "When it is, I'll stop."

"You son of a bitch. How can you respond like that to your own little girl?"

"She didn't hear me."

"She did."

"Did you, Debbie?"

"When is it Christmas?"

"See what you've done," Claire said, and Rich watched the two of them walk into the other room. Claire seemed to have guessed what had crossed his mind:

with their stuff packed it was an opportunity to call the whole thing off once and for all. To make a break for it. And guessed, too, that the fumigation might be, in his mind, some sort of complication to that master plan.

It wasn't rational, his reactions. He and the girls would be out the house for two and a half days and then be back. Yet there was something intimate about being forced out like refugees and also about staying together in a motel. Especially as Debbie was so excited about the latter. It would be a hell of a cruel way to end it all. They were splurging on a nice motel–hotel, actually–near Disneyland and had secret plans to take Debbie to Disneyland. It would be her first visit. Or would be if the rain let up.

Actually, the thought hadn't really occurred to Rich prior to the packing. Going through his books had started him wondering if maybe he was giving up too much to remain married. He didn't like making a living. He didn't like teaching. Without a family–even with child support–he'd have more time for his photography. He'd still have a living to make of course,but he'd be free to travel more. Photographers need to. But more deeply it wasn't just a problem of a lack of time and movement, it was a problem of a lack of mental space. An artist needs to be free to just sit and stare out a window, travel or no travel. Further, he didn't love Claire the way he used to. He loved Debbie more than anything in the world, including photography. But it wasn't like that, life wasn't. You can't give up your vocation, not for anything. It was not at present his vocation but someday it might be, could be. Yet it had been so nice in the bathroom with Claire–they'd never done it on the toilet seat–that he couldn't help but feel at the same time it was the way things were meant to be and all these other thoughts he had were just that, thoughts. Pictures. Brought to a head by the pending fumigation.

Not pending. Imminent now.

"We'll put this stuff in your car," Claire said. "Debbie can ride with me."

"Okay."

"Where's Daddy going?" Debbie put in.

"We're going to follow him to our motel."

"Oh. With Trix?"

"Yes."

"Okay."

Rich was still picturing the tent and all their stuff under it. The circus performers were dead as were the animals. It made him want to scream.

"I'll drive slow, sweetheart. We're going to Disneyland."

"Rich."

"Disneyland, Daddy?"

"She might as well know."

"What if it doesn't stop raining?"

"It will."

Claire smiled. "What, you're a weatherman now, too?"

"Too?"

What was he? He was a husband, a father, a son, a teacher, a photographer. He'd get his opportunity.

"I don't want to see it, do you?" he said to Claire.

"What?"

"The tent."

"Why?"

"Do you?"

"I don't care one way or the other. It's just a big tent. I've seen them before. I can imagine it."

"That's exactly the problem. We won't see it, will we? We'll come back late Friday, when it's dark, okay? After everyone else has already returned, okay?"

"Yes, honey, okay. We'll wait until it's completely dark. Pitch black. You're so sentimental, now."

"I know."

"Don't worry." She shook her head, bemused. "Now let's go. It's almost time."

www.ingramcontent.com/pod-product-compliance
Lightning Source LLC
Chambersburg PA
CBHW070751180626
46818CB00007B/3071